Thistle & Thread

Katherine Kuehnel

This is a work of fiction. Names, characters, places, and incidents are the product of the author's imagination or are used fictitiously. Any resemblance to actual events, locales, or persons, living or dead, is purely coincidental.

ISBN: 9798299369359
 Cover design by Katherine Kuehnel
 Edited by Katherine Kuehnel

Printed in the United States of America

First Edition, October 2025

For Grace and Ashlyn—

This story grew from quiet places,
but it's your laughter, your questions, your boundless wonder
that gave it a voice.

Your hearts are lanterns,
your laughter is spellwork,
and your love teaches me—every day—
that softness is not weakness.
It's wonder.

May you always believe in magic,
especially your own.

-Mom

❦ *Thistle & Thread: The Quiet Bloom Mix*

A playlist for soft hearts, bookshop spells, and love that stays.

1. **"The Archer"** – Taylor Swift

2. **"Cosmic Love"** – Florence + the Machine

3. **"Cherry Wine (Live)"** – Hozier

4. **"Light Years"** – The National

5. **"The Night We Met"** – Lord Huron

6. **"Turning Page"** – Sleeping at Last

7. **"I Know The End"** – Phoebe Bridgers

8. **"Like Real People Do"** – Hozier

9. **"Meet Me in the Woods"** – Lord Huron

10. **"Canyon Moon"** – Harry Styles

11. **"A Safe Place to Land"** – Sara Bareilles & John Legend

12. **"Daylight"** – Taylor Swift

13. **"All is Found"** – Kacey Musgraves

14. **"Saturn"** – Sleeping at Last

15. **"Evergreen"** – YEBBA

16. **"Shake It Out"** – Florence + the Machine

17. **"Roslyn"** – Bon Iver & St. Vincent

18. **"Work Song"** – Hozier

19. **"This Is On Me"** – Ben Abraham & Sara Bareilles

20. **"Lover, You Should've Come Over"** – Jeff Buckley

21. **"August"** – Taylor Swift

Prologue

Chapter 1: The First Leaf Falls

Chapter 2: Tea and Tangled Roots

Chapter 3: The Long Quiet Shelf

Chapter 4: Root Memory

Chapter 5: The Lantern Market

Chapter 6: A Cup Meant for Me

Chapter 7: Rootbound

Chapter 8: The Memory Jar

Chapter 9: The Path Between

Chapter 10: Heartbrew and Honeylight

Chapter 11: The Seed Grows Quietly

Chapter 12: Inkroot and Echoes

Author's Note

About the Author

✦ Coming Soon from Katherine Kuehnel

The Honeybrew Café

"Love does not always arrive like lightning.

Sometimes it drifts in like falling leaves—

soft, golden, and impossible to stop."

Prologue

In Faerrow, tales do not commence with the sudden crash of thunder, a jarring clamor that demands attention. No, they ease into existence with a softer touch, a gentler breath.

They begin with warmth, the kind that seeps into your bones and eases the tension from your shoulders. The kind that wraps around you like a familiar embrace, inviting you to settle in, to stay awhile. It's the warmth of a hearth fire that has burned steadily for generations, of a sun-kissed blanket spread out beneath an ancient tree. It's the warmth of a kettle left to steep, the heat of it rising like a whispered secret, carrying with it the promise of comfort, of solace.

A name spoken gently, with the same tenderness one might use to coax a shy creature from its hiding spot. It's not a shout or a command, but an invitation, a recognition of the soul that bears that name. It's the sound of home, of belonging, of roots that run deep and true.

A door that never fully closed, always slightly ajar, a silent sentinel that bears witness to the comings and goings of life. It's not an oversight or a mistake, but a deliberate choice, a quiet welcome. It's a testament to the open hearts of those who dwell within, to the warmth that spills out, beckoning, enticing, enfolding.

Magic lives here, but it's not the flashy, showy kind. It's not loud or sharp, not the type that demands attention or craves admiration. No, it's quiet and slow, the kind that waits, that bides its time. It's the kind that roots, that sinks deep into the earth, that grows steadily, patiently, inevitably. It's the kind that remembers who you are when you forget, that whispers your name when you've lost your way, that guides you home when you've wandered far.

The wind doesn't carry omens here, doesn't howl prophecies or scream warnings. The rain doesn't fall with purpose, doesn't drench with intent, or soak with meaning. But the trees, they lean in when something is beginning. They rustle their leaves, creak their branches, whisper their ancient wisdom. And the books, if you're listening, will hum. They'll thrum with the echoes of stories past, with the anticipation of tales yet to come. They'll sing softly, a chorus of history and hope, of magic and mystery.

This is not the story of a hero, of a grand quest, or a daring deed. It's not the story of a savior, of a champion, of a brave soul seeking glory or acclaim. No, it's something softer, something gentler, something infinitely more precious.

It is the story of a girl, of a heart that beats with quiet courage, of a spirit that shines with steady light. It is the story of a grove, of a sanctuary, of a haven that hums with ancient magic, that whispers with sacred secrets. And it is the story of a love that never asked to be proven, that never demanded to be tested, that only wanted to be kept, to be cherished, to be held close and true.

Chapter 1: The First Leaf Falls

The first leaf fell sometime before dawn, descending in a silent, solitary dance. It landed with a gentle tap on the cobblestones, a harbinger of the changing season.

I notice it as I open the shutters of *Thistle & Thread,* my little bookshop nestled at the edge of Faerrow's moss-lined square. The leaf lay on the ground, crimson against the gray stone, curled like a secret waiting to be whispered. I pause, my hand still on the window latch, and let out a breath that misted in the cool morning air. The scent of autumn—cloves and woodsmoke, damp earth and distant bonfires—hangs heavily, hinting at the transformations to come.

"It's starting," I murmur to Whisker, who sat perched on the windowsill like a shadow stitched in velvet. His eyes, green as the deepest forest glades, watch me intently.

Whisker flicks his tail in agreement, his fur ruffling slightly with the motion. He always knows when the shift comes. When summer sighs its last warm breath and lets autumn take the lead. In Faerrow, the change isn't loud—it's a hush, a thickening of the air, a quiet symphony of scent and sensation that speaks of endings and enchantments.

Inside, the shop is already dressed for the season. The center table, usually a simple display of new arrivals, now overflows with books on harvest lore and hearth magic, stacked like pumpkins in a patch, each cover a promise of stories and spells. A string of tiny lanterns shaped like acorns and mushrooms glows amber across the archway, casting warm, inviting light over the worn spines and faded titles. Someone less sentimental might say I overdid it, but I've always believed books deserve to be celebrated the same way people do— especially the old ones. Especially the lonely ones that sit on my shelves, waiting for just the right person to come along and give them life again.

I brew my first pot of spiced plum tea, the scent curling through the shelves like a welcome spell, inviting the day and its possibilities. Outside, the village is waking slowly. Mr. Wrenly opens his bakery across the square, the delicious aroma of fresh bread and pastries wafting through the air as he hums about cinnamon buns and apple tarts. Fae children skip along the cobbles with scarves trailing like comet tails, their laughter echoing off the ancient stones. Their wings, usually free and fluttering, are tucked beneath knit cloaks, a sure sign that the chill of autumn has begun to set in.

I step outside to hang the sign: **First Leaf Festival – Readings, Rituals, & Recipes All Week**. I adjust the angle twice, then again, my fingers lingering on the polished wood as I try to get it just right. Whisker, having grown bored of my perfectionism, leaps down from the windowsill and trots toward the flower barrels at the corner, his tail held high like a banner.

"Not too far," I call after him, my voice carrying a note of affectionate exasperation. He ignores me in the way only cats and fae do, disappearing around the corner with a flick of his tail.

I go back inside, rearranging the front table for the third time, my hands moving books from one stack to another as I try to find the perfect balance of color and theme. The shop bell jingles once—then twice more in quick succession, interrupting my careful arrangement.

Not a customer.

Whisker is back.

And he isn't alone.

The second chime comes from the quiet step of a stranger.

I look up, my hands stilling on the worn cover of an old tome.

A fae male stands in the doorway, tall and haloed in mist. His coat is dusted with dew, and small leaf fragments cling to his sleeves like stubborn memories, hinting at a journey through forests and fields. His hair—an untamed shade of sunlit wheat—curls damply around his collar, framing a face that is both striking and kind. Slung over one shoulder is a satchel, patched with dried moss and tiny pressed flowers, a testament to his travels and the stories he carries with him.

And at his feet: Whisker. Purring.

The traitor.

"Apologies," the stranger says, his voice low and unhurried, like the deep hum of a summer evening. "He led me in."

Whisker glances up smugly, his green eyes gleaming with satisfaction as if to say, *You're welcome.*

I blink, taken aback by the unexpected visitor and my cat's sudden change in allegiance. "He usually doesn't do that. Lead people in," I say, my words tinged with a mix of surprise and curiosity.

"Then I suppose I should be honored," the man replies, a soft smile playing at the corners of his mouth.

The man's smile is gentle, but his eyes are brighter than the usual amber of our kind—closer to the green-gold of ginkgo leaves in late October, when the world is a tapestry of fiery hues and faded gold. He steps forward with care, his gaze roaming the shelves as if he were trying not to disturb something sacred, something fragile and precious that lay hidden among the books.

"I'm looking for something," he says, running a hand through his rain-damp curls, the gesture both casual and thoughtful. "Though I'm not quite sure what."

I give a half-smile, my eyes reflecting the warm light of the lanterns overhead. "You've come to the right place, then. We specialize in uncertain needs."

"Do you now?" He tilts his head, intrigued, his eyes sparkling with curiosity. "That's a rare specialty."

I gesture to the shop, my hand sweeping in a graceful arc that encompasses the shelves and the stories they hold. "The books know things. They find people, not the other way around."

"Ah," he says, as if this makes perfect sense, as if he understands the magic that lives within the pages of my books. "Then I'll let them decide."

8

I watch him drift to a nearby shelf, his fingers brushing the spines with reverence, as if each one holds a secret waiting to be revealed. Whisker winds around his legs once more before disappearing behind the poetry section, his matchmaking apparently complete, his duty done.

I tuck a loose strand of hair behind my ear, my gaze following the stranger as he moves through my shop. "You're not from Faerrow."

He glances at me over his shoulder, his eyes meeting mine with a look that is both open and guarded, like a door left slightly ajar. "No. I've just returned. I was born here—left long ago."

"Welcome home, then," I say gently, my voice soft with understanding and warmth.

His eyes soften in response, the green-gold depths reflecting the glow of the lanterns. "Thank you. I'm Aurelian."

"Elowen," I reply, my name a whisper on my lips, a secret shared in the quiet of my shop. "And the cat is Whisker, though he has many secret names."

Aurelian chuckles, the sound warm and inviting, like the first sip of mulled wine on a cold winter's night. "Don't we all?"

He pauses in front of a worn, leather-bound volume titled *Rootwork and Rainwater: Folklore for Fading Seasons*. As he touches it, the air shimmers faintly—just enough for me to notice, just enough to tell me that the book has chosen him, that it holds something he needs, something he has been searching for without even knowing it.

"Looks like the shop's already found something for you," I say, my voice tinged with satisfaction and a hint of pride.

He cradles the book as if it were alive, as if it held a heartbeat and a soul, as if it were a treasure to be cherished and protected. "Then I suppose I'll stay awhile."

Chapter 2: Tea and Tangled Roots

The kettle sings softly in the back room, a gentle melody that weaves through the air like an enchanted thread. Steam unfurls in delicate tendrils, dancing in the soft glow of the late afternoon light. I pour the water, a cascade of heat, over a hand-blended mix of dried apple, chamomile, and cinnamon bark, the scent immediately filling the room with a comforting warmth. I stir it slowly, clockwise, as if winding a clock that measures moments rather than hours. Leaning down, I whisper a quiet charm, a secret lullaby that seals in comfort and clarity, making the brew more than just a simple tea.

Some spells don't need words. Some live in rituals, in the silent poetry of everyday actions. They reside in the way I steep tea, allowing the leaves to unfurl like tiny stories in the hot water. They hide in the way I open a book, the spine crackling like an ancient greeting. They even dwell in the way I light a lantern just before dusk, the strike of the match a small, defiant shout against the encroaching darkness.

11

Out in the shop, Aurelian wanders with a gentle curiosity, his footsteps soft as if he walks on hallowed ground. He moves like someone who doesn't want to disturb the dust motes, those tiny particles dancing in the fading sunlight. His steps are careful, deliberate, respectful, as if he understands that every object here has a story, a soul. I watch from the doorway for a moment, the tea tray balanced in my hands, before clearing my throat gently. It's not a reprimand, just a soft announcement of my presence.

"Careful with that one," I warn as he reaches for a narrow volume bound in bark, its spine rough and gnarled like an ancient tree. "It recites seasonal poetry. Loudly," I add, a small smile playing on my lips.

He freezes, hand halfway to the spine, fingers hovering as if caught in an invisible web. "Noted," he says, his voice barely above a whisper, a conspiratorial tone that makes me smile wider.

I motion toward the reading nook near the hearth, where two mismatched armchairs wait like old friends, their cushions worn and welcoming. Aurelian takes a seat, the bark-spined book now wisely left untouched on the shelf. Whisker is already curled in the corner, one eye half-lidded but watchful, his tail twitching occasionally as he dreams of chasing shadows.

I set down the tea tray, the porcelain cups clinking softly against the wooden surface. Handing him the mug with a crescent moon painted on the side, I say, "This one's called Hearthbrew. For when things feel heavy."

Aurelian accepts it with both hands, cradling the mug as if it holds something precious. He takes a slow sip, his eyes fluttering shut for just a moment, a soft sigh escaping his lips.

"That tastes like memory," he murmurs, his voice barely audible. "And quiet things. Safe things," he adds, his eyes still closed, as if he's drifting on a sea of tranquility.

"I always let the blend decide," I reply, my voice soft but firm. "Tea knows more than it lets on," I continue, a small smile tugging at the corners of my mouth.

He opens his eyes again, meeting mine, his gaze steady and searching. "You say that like it's not a joke," he says, a hint of amusement in his voice.

"It's not," I reply, my expression serious. There's no laughter in my voice, no hint of playfulness. Just a simple truth, stated plainly.

13

Something passes between us then—something gentle, but rooted. As if the tea had brewed not just leaves, but a possibility, a connection that was always there, waiting to be acknowledged.

Outside, the drizzle has thickened to a steady fall, each drop pattering against the windows like a drumbeat no one dances to anymore. The world outside is a symphony of grays, the rain a monotonous melody that lulls the city into a state of quiet introspection. Inside, the fire pops, the wood crackling and hissing as it surrenders to the flames. The scent of cinnamon hangs in the air like a lullaby, a warm, comforting embrace that makes the shop feel like a sanctuary, a haven from the storm outside.

"So," Aurelian says after a moment, his voice breaking the comfortable silence that had settled between us. "What exactly do you do here, besides craft emotionally sentient beverages and rescue books with opinions?" he asks, a playful smile tugging at his lips.

I laugh, the sound light and honey-warm, a melody that dances in the air like the steam from the tea. "I keep stories alive," I say, my voice filled with a quiet passion. "I bind them when they fall apart, stitching their pages back together like a healer mending broken bones," I explain, my hands mimicking the act of binding, my fingers

14

weaving an invisible thread. "I find homes for the ones no one remembers, the tales that have been forgotten, the voices that have been silenced," I continue, my voice filled with a fierce determination.

"And the magic?" Aurelian asks, his voice barely above a whisper, as if he's afraid to disturb the sacred atmosphere of the shop.

"It's... subtle," I say, choosing my words carefully, as if each one is a precious stone that needs to be handled with care. "I don't do big spells. I listen," I explain, my voice filled with a quiet reverence. "Books speak in whispers, and magic does too, if you let it," I say, my eyes meeting his, a silent understanding passing between us.

He sips again, his brow furrowed in thought, his eyes distant as if he's lost in a world of his own. "That's rare these days," he murmurs, his voice filled with a soft longing.

"You mean the loud kind of magic is louder now," I say, my voice filled with a quiet understanding. I know what he means, the way the world has changed, the way magic has become a spectacle, a show, rather than a quiet, sacred thing.

"Yes," he says, a pause following his words, a silence filled with unspoken thoughts. "But I prefer the quieter sort," he admits, his voice filled with a soft sincerity.

15

"Then you're in the right place," I say, a small smile playing on my lips. This shop, this sanctuary, is a haven for the quiet, the subtle, the forgotten. It's a place where whispers are louder than shouts, where the rustle of a page is more powerful than any spell.

Aurelian sets his mug down, the porcelain clinking softly against the wooden table. "I study root systems," he says, his voice filled with a quiet passion. "Seasonal botany. The way magic settles into soil and sleeps," he explains, his hands mimicking the act of digging, his fingers buried in invisible earth.

"You're a listener, too," I say, my voice filled with a soft understanding. I recognize the look in his eyes, the quiet intensity, the subtle passion. It's the look of someone who understands the power of silence, the magic of listening.

He looks at me then—not past me, not through me, but right at me. His gaze is steady, unwavering, as if he sees me, truly sees me, for the first time. "I try to be," he says, his voice filled with a quiet sincerity.

The silence that follows isn't awkward. It's soft. Spacious. Like the shop is expanding to give us room, to give us space to breathe, to think, to be. It's a comfortable silence, a shared understanding, a mutual respect.

"You said you just returned," I say finally, my voice breaking the silence that had settled between us. "Where have you been?" I ask, my voice filled with a gentle curiosity.

"Wandering," he says, his voice distant, as if he's recalling a memory, a journey filled with sights and sounds and scents. "Studying. I spent years in the Ember Glade archives, buried under mountains of parchment, surrounded by the scent of ancient ink and dust," he explains, his eyes distant, as if he's lost in a world of his own. "Then in the southern grove colonies, where the air is thick with the scent of blooming flowers and the hum of magic is a constant melody," he continues, his voice filled with a soft longing. "I haven't stayed anywhere longer than a season until now," he admits, his voice filled with a quiet sincerity.

"And why here?" I ask, unable to stop myself. The question slips out before I can catch it, a curious bird escaping its cage.

Aurelian's fingers trace the rim of his mug, his gaze distant, as if he's searching for an answer, a reason, a truth. "I remembered something about Faerrow," he says, his voice filled with a soft nostalgia. "About how it smells when the leaves turn, the scent of autumn filling the air like a promise," he explains, his eyes meeting mine, a silent understanding passing between us. "About the way quiet doesn't mean lonely here," he adds, his voice filled with a quiet sincerity.

I don't know what to say to that. His words are like a spell, a charm, a whisper of magic that leaves me speechless, breathless, at a loss for words.

So I say, "Would you like to see the back room?" The words come out in a rush, a tumble of syllables that fill the silence that had settled between us.

He raises a brow, his expression a mixture of surprise and amusement.

"For the restoration table," I clarify, my cheeks warming, a soft blush spreading across my face. "There's an old book I'm trying to rebind. It won't stop humming," I explain, my voice filled with a mixture of exasperation and affection.

He stands, a smile playing on his lips, his eyes sparkling with amusement. "Lead the way," he says, his voice filled with a quiet eagerness.

The back room of *Thistle & Thread* is smaller than the shop front, a cozy nook filled with the scent of beeswax and pressed petals. The air is thick with the smell of old parchment and ancient ink, a symphony of scents that tell a story of their own. There are stacks of worn tomes, their spines cracked and faded, their pages yellowed with age. Vials of powdered ink line the shelves, their contents shimmering like captured stardust. Feathers in glass jars catch the light, their colors a dance of hues, a whispered secret shared between the sun and the glass. A single narrow window is streaked with fog, the world outside a blur of grays and greens, a painting seen through a veil of mist.

In the center of the room stands the restoration table, a wooden beast scarred with the marks of time and use. Upon it lies a book bound in cracked leather, its cover worn and faded, its edges frayed like an ancient tapestry. The book is gently vibrating, a soft hum filling the air like the whisper of a thousand bees.

Aurelian steps closer, his footsteps soft, his eyes fixed on the book as if drawn by an invisible force. "It's singing," he murmurs, his voice filled with a mixture of awe and curiosity.

"It's stubborn," I say, a small smile playing on my lips as I place a hand on the book, the humming vibrating against my palm like a purring cat. "It only opens during the autumn equinox, and only for someone it trusts," I explain, my voice filled with a mixture of exasperation and affection.

"Have you tried asking?" Aurelian asks, his voice filled with a quiet sincerity, his eyes meeting mine, a silent understanding passing between us.

I blink, taken aback by the simplicity of his suggestion. "Asking?" I repeat, the word a foreign concept, a strange idea that had never occurred to me before.

He leans forward, one hand on the table, his fingers splayed against the wooden surface. Whispering softly, as if sharing a secret with an old friend, he asks, "Would you let me read you?"

The humming stops.

The book creaks open, its pages rustling like the wings of a butterfly, a soft sigh escaping its depths as if it had been holding its breath for centuries, waiting for this moment, waiting for this question, waiting for him.

I stare, my eyes wide with disbelief, my mouth agape with shock. "You charmed it," I whisper, my voice filled with a mixture of awe and admiration.

"No," he says softly, his voice filled with a quiet sincerity, his eyes meeting mine, a silent understanding passing between us. "I think it remembered me," he says, his voice filled with a soft wonder, as if he's recalling a memory, a connection, a truth that had been buried deep within him, waiting to be awakened.

We stand side by side, our shoulders brushing, our breaths synchronized, as if we are two parts of a whole, two halves of a story that had been waiting to be told. Reading in silence, our eyes scanning the ancient text, our minds lost in a world of words and whispers, of magic and memories, of truths and tales that had been forgotten, waiting to be remembered, waiting to be reborn.

Somewhere in the shop, the bell jingles, its melody a soft echo in the silence that had settled between us. But no one comes in, the world outside a distant dream, a faraway reality that had no place in this sanctuary, this haven, this temple of tales and truths.

The tea has gone cold, its surface a still pond reflecting the dance of the flames in the hearth. But the connection between us has

21

steeped into something deeper, something stronger, something that transcends time and space, something that binds us like the words in an ancient tome, like the roots of an ancient tree, like the magic that settles into soil and sleeps, waiting to be awakened, waiting to be remembered, waiting to be reborn.

Chapter 3: The Long Quiet Shelf

The rain had stopped sometime during our reading, its persistent patter fading into a silence that we hadn't noticed. It was only when Aurelian gently shut the humming book, his fingers lingering on the worn cover, and tilted his head toward the window that the change in weather became apparent. Outside, the cobblestones glistened under the moon's silver gaze, slick with the memory of rain and the soft glow of moonlight. A tendril of mist drifted lazily down the narrow lane, wrapping my small bookshop in a breath of tranquility, as if the world itself had hushed to listen to the stories within.

"I didn't mean to stay so long," Aurelian said, his voice a low rumble, almost apologetic, yet tinged with a warmth that made the words feel more like a confession than an apology. He looked at me, his eyes reflecting the gentle light of the shop, and a slight smile played on his lips.

I glanced at the clock perched high on the wall, though I didn't need its hands to tell me what my body already knew. Time had slipped away, unnoticed and unheeded, as it often did when lost in the pages of a good book. Hours had passed in what felt like mere moments, folding softly into the shape of something precious and worth keeping. I turned my gaze back to Aurelian, his eyes soft with the remnants of shared stories.

"You weren't in the way," I said, my fingers brushing across the leather-bound book that now lay still and faintly warm on the table. "The shop likes you." I said it with a quiet certainty, because the shop itself was a living entity with its own preferences and moods.

He raised an eyebrow, a playful glint in his eyes. "Is that a good thing?" He asked, a hint of amusement in his voice.

I smiled, a small, teasing curve of my lips. "For now," I said, my eyes sparkling with mirth.

He chuckled, a sound that was deep and genuine, and leaned back slightly on the edge of the restoration table. His hands were tucked into the pockets of his moss-colored coat, the fabric worn and soft with age. His presence felt like something my little shop hadn't held in a long time—a quiet companion who didn't try to fill the silence with unnecessary words, but rather sat beside it and listened, as if the silence itself had a story to tell.

24

After a pause, Aurelian spoke again, his voice thoughtful. "You mentioned a shelf," his eyes searching mine. "One that's... quiet?"

I tilted my head, caught off guard by the question. My brows furrowed slightly as I considered his words. "The Long Quiet Shelf," I said, voice barely above a whisper, as if sharing a secret. "It's not officially called that, but it's what I call it."

His curiosity was piqued. "What's on it?" he asked, his eyes alight with interest.

I paused, fingers tracing the grain of the wooden table as I thought about how to explain. "Books no one checks out," I said finally. "Stories too gentle or strange for passing eyes. Mostly fae-written works about things no one remembers how to name. A few are written in disappearing ink, their words fading like whispers in the wind."

Aurelian's eyes lit up with wonder, like a child hearing about a hidden treasure. "Can I see?" he asked, his voice filled with a reverence that made my heart flutter.

I hesitated, not because I didn't want to share, but because the shelf was a kind of secret. A little magic of my own, hidden away in

25

the depths of the shop. And yet, there was something about his request, something gentle and sincere, that made me want to share my secret with him. He had asked not with the greed of someone wanting to possess, but with the curiosity of someone wanting to understand.

"Alright," I said, my voice soft yet firm. "But you have to promise to put your hands behind your back unless invited."

He grinned, a boyish charm that made his eyes crinkle at the corners. "Scout's honor," he said, already tucking his hands behind his back in a playful gesture of surrender.

I led him through the main shop, our footsteps quiet on the worn wooden floor. We passed the display window where lanterns now glowed soft gold against the encroaching dusk, casting long shadows that danced and flickered with each step. We passed the history shelves, tall and proud, their books bearing the weight of time and memory. We passed the cookbooks, their pages stained with the ghosts of meals past, and the dream journals, their covers adorned with symbols that shimmered in the half-light.

Finally, we reached the very back corner of the shop. Here, beneath a crooked beam and beside a cracked-glass window, stood a narrow bookshelf made of aged oak and rune-carved nails. A single cobweb hung like lace from the upper corner, undisturbed and delicate. The Long Quiet Shelf stood before us, its secrets whispered in the dust that clung to the books' spines.

I lit the nearby wall lantern with a whispered flick of my fingers, the flame springing to life with a soft hum. The light shimmered soft and blue, a hue reserved for gentle things, for stories that needed coaxing to be told.

"There," I said, stepping back and gesturing towards the shelf. "Go slow."

Aurelian obeyed, his eyes moving over the spines with a reverence that made my heart ache. He read aloud, his voice barely above a whisper, as if the very words were sacred. *"The Shape of Silence." "Petaltruth." "How Stars Sleep."* He paused, his fingers hovering over a book with no title, its spine bare and unadorned. "This one doesn't have a title," he said, his voice filled with wonder.

"It doesn't want one," I said, my voice gentle. "At least, not yet."

He crouched down, inspecting a slender volume bound in green-dyed bark. He fingers traced the rough edges, his eyes filled with awe. "This looks like it was grown," he said, his voice barely above a whisper.

I nodded, a small smile playing on my lips. "It was," I said. "A sentient vine wrote it over the course of one equinox cycle. It wove its story into the very fibers of the bark, a tale of growth and change as old as time itself."

He let out a soft breath of wonder, his eyes scanning the shelf with renewed curiosity. "This shelf is full of lost magic," his voice filled with a reverence that made my heart swell.

I nodded, my eyes soft with memories. "It holds the kind of stories that don't shout," I said. "They wait, patient and unassuming, for the right person to come along and listen."

He turned towards me then, slower than before, something quiet and intense in his gaze. "You're one of them, aren't you?" he asked, voice barely above a whisper.

I blinked, surprised by the question. "One of what?" I asked, my voice filled with confusion.

"Stories that wait," Aurelian said, his eyes never leaving mine. There was a sincerity in his gaze, a depth that made my breath catch in my throat.

For a moment, the world seemed to hold its breath, the air thick with unspoken words and shared secrets. Then I looked away, my eyes flickering to the shelf of forgotten stories. "I've never been very good at loud," I said, my voice quiet yet firm. It was a confession, a truth laid bare in the quiet of the shop.

His voice was gentle, filled with understanding. "Loud is overrated," he said, his eyes never leaving my face.

We stood there for a long beat, the hush between us not uncomfortable, but delicate—like a leaf floating in still water, its journey unhurried and unforced. The silence was a living thing, a testament to the stories that filled the shop, to the magic that lingered in the air.

Whisker meowed softly behind us, clearly done with secrets and shared silences. He nudged Aurelian's ankle with an impatient tail swipe, his amber eyes filled with a feline impatience that brooked no argument. He padded towards the front of the shop, his tail held high, clearly expecting us to follow.

He smiled, a soft curve of his lips that made his eyes crinkle at the corners. "I think I'm being dismissed," he said, his voice filled with amusement.

I chuckled, my eyes soft with affection as I watched Whisker's retreating form. "He's subtle like that," I said, my voice tinged with sarcasm.

We followed Whisker back to the entryway, our footsteps soft on the worn wooden floor. Here, the last hint of twilight spilled amber light across the floorboards, casting long shadows that danced and flickered with each step. He paused near the door, his hands brushing mist from his sleeves, the fabric damp from the lingering fog. The pressed flowers on his satchel had shifted, one tiny sunflower now lay just beneath the clasp, fresh despite the damp, a small burst of color against the worn leather.

I reached out before I realized I was doing it, my fingers grazing the petal, the touch light and almost tentative. "Here," I said, voice soft. "You've got... a stowaway."

He didn't move, his body still as he let my fingers linger on the sunflower. I looked up, his gaze already waiting, already knowing. There was a softness in his eyes, a warmth that made my heart flutter.

"Lian," I said, trying out the name for the first time aloud. It came out softer than I intended, a whisper of sound that hung in the air between us. Private. Intimate.

30

His breath caught slightly at the sound, his eyes never leaving mine. There was a promise in his gaze, a silent vow that made my heart ache with longing.

"You'll come back?" I asked, voice barely above a whisper, breath held captive in my chest.

His voice was firm, filled with a conviction that left no room for doubt. "I don't think I could stay away," he said.

The bell above the door jingled softly as he stepped into the night, his silhouette dissolving into the moon-kissed fog. The mist embraced him, wrapping him in its ethereal embrace, as if the very night itself was welcoming him home.

I stood in the doorway a moment longer, hand resting against the frame, fingers tracing the grain of the wood. Behind me, Whisker purred, the sound soft and content, like a spell well-cast, a magic woven into the very fabric of the shop. The night was quiet, the world hushed, as if holding its breath in anticipation of the stories yet to be told, the secrets yet to be shared. And I stood in the heart of it, my shop a beacon of light in the darkness, a sanctuary for the stories that waited, for the magic that lingered, for the quiet companions who listened to the silence and found beauty in its song.

31

Chapter 4: Root Memory

I didn't come back for her. Not initially, at least.

The truth is, I returned because the very air seemed to have shifted, as if the world itself was whispering secrets on the wind. The leaves in the northern groves had begun their transformation earlier than usual this year, painting the landscape with hues of gold and crimson. The frostroot bloomed suddenly, unexpectedly, their delicate petals unfurling like crystalline whispers against the earth. And the dreams I had long ago pressed into the soil, dreams I thought were silent and forgotten, started to stir once more, their murmurs echoing through my restless nights.

But if I'm honest with myself—and Elowen has a way of drawing honesty out of me, even in the quietest of moments—I stayed because of her. Because the instant I stepped into that quaint little bookshop, with its scent of aged parchment and fresh ink, and she turned to face me with smudges of ink on her fingertips and the aroma of tea wafting through the air, something within me shifted. The root

I had buried deep in the heart of this village a decade ago began to reach for the surface, yearning for the light.

Faerrow, at first glance, hadn't changed much. The cobbled square remained the same, each stone worn smooth by the passage of time and countless footsteps. The lazy rhythm of the hours ticked by as they always had, unhurried and unconcerned with the world beyond the village borders. There was an almost tangible sense that Faerrow had made a pact long ago to operate just slightly out of sync with the rest of the world, content in its own quiet pace.

But the grove had changed. The trees seemed to stand a little taller, their branches stretching out like welcoming arms. The undergrowth was denser, richer, as if the very essence of the place had deepened in my absence. And so had I. I was no longer the same person who had left all those years ago.

I've always been a traveler, not out of some grand ambition, but out of an insatiable restlessness. I told myself that I moved from season to season because the work needed me, that the soil didn't demand permanence, only presence. But the truth, the one I've been avoiding for so long, is that I moved because I didn't know how to stay. Because no one had ever asked me to.

The first time I saw her, she wasn't looking at me. She was standing outside her bookshop, barefoot despite the chill in the air, her cardigan slipping off one shoulder as she adjusted a crooked sign. Her cat, Whisker, wove around her ankles with an air of ownership, as if he were the true master of the street. Perhaps he was.

There was something about her posture, a groundedness that seemed to radiate from her very being. She didn't need the village to make space for her; she had already carved it out herself, gently but with a certainty that was almost palpable. It was as if she belonged there, not just in the physical sense, but in a way that was woven into the very fabric of the place.

Then she looked up, her eyes meeting mine, and I felt it. Not magic, not some grand calling, just... stillness. A profound, resonant stillness, as if I had finally stopped moving without even realizing that I had needed to.

The books in her shop seemed to recognize me before I did. I reached for one—a volume bound in bark, its pages filled with seasonal lore—and it hummed in my hands, familiar and comforting. It was like a child tugging at a parent's sleeve, urging me to look, to remember. You forgot this, it seemed to say.

34

And when she offered me tea, something deep within me ached. Because no one makes tea like that unless they understand the importance of silence, unless they know that stillness is not merely the absence of sound, but the presence of intention. She brewed it with a reverence that was almost sacred, as if each cup were a small blessing.

And I drank it like someone who had been waiting, perhaps without even knowing it, to be invited back into their own story.

That night, I didn't unpack my satchel. Not because I planned to leave again, but because I didn't know how to unpack somewhere I hadn't yet been asked to stay. But I did press a memory bulb into the soil behind the shop, quietly and without words. A tiny spell, a root for something I wasn't quite ready to name.

Not yet.

Chapter 5: The Lantern Market

The morning of the Lantern Market arrived on soft, silent feet, wrapped in a cinnamon-scented fog that seemed to muffle the usual sounds of the waking town. The sun, a hazy glow behind the thick mist, cast a warm and drowsy light over the cobblestone streets, as if nature herself was slowly stirring from a long slumber.

I knew it before I even opened my eyes—something in the air had shifted, like the almost imperceptible change that occurs when a page turns softly in a very old, very beloved book. Whisker confirmed my suspicions by jumping onto my chest with a soft *thud*, his yowl a clear declaration of *You're late for nothing, but I'm judging you anyway, female.*

I blinked up at him, his green eyes staring into mine with an intensity that only cats can muster. "You're lucky you're cute, Whisker," I murmured, my voice still heavy with sleep. He blinked slowly in return, utterly unbothered by my mild rebuke, his tail flicking lazily behind him.

By the time I made it downstairs, the scent of the Lantern Market had already begun infiltrating my small bookshop. The air was filled with the aroma of roasting chestnuts and fresh caramel, a sweet and comforting smell that was unique to this time of year. Faerrow only smelled like this once a year—during the three magical days of the Lantern Market, when the town square filled with stalls, laughter echoed through the streets, and a peculiar kind of magic, meant only for delight, danced in the air.

I lit the spell-lanterns that hung above the door, each one humming a soft note as it warmed, their glow casting a cozy light over the shop. They would keep the bookshop inviting while I stepped out, and anyone who wandered in would know, without being told, to treat the space with gentleness and respect. I left a note for any curious customers on the counter—*Back by dusk. Feel free to browse. Don't feed the cat anything caffeinated. —E—*before donning my scarf and grabbing my woven basket.

Whisker was already perched in the display window like a watchful gargoyle, his eyes following my every move as I stepped into the crisp, honey-colored air. Outside, the world shimmered with an almost ethereal beauty. Stalls lined the cobblestones, each one glowing with warm lanternlight despite the daylight, their owners calling out to passersby, enticing them with their wares. Some of the lanterns floated above the booths, swaying gently like sleepy fireflies on a summer's eve. Others glowed from within carved pumpkins, their flickering lights dancing to unheard songs that seemed to whisper through the air.

Children darted between the displays, their fingers sticky with caramel apples, laughter trailing behind them like ribbons. Someone played a lute off-key near the bakery, the notes blending with the chatter and laughter to create a symphony unique to the Lantern Market. Mr. Wrenly, the baker, had a line stretching down the square for his famous plum tarts, the scent of their warm, fruity filling wafting through the air and making my mouth water.

I drifted past a stall selling spiced pear wine, the merchant offering samples to those who passed by, and another stacked high with scarves dyed in moonwater, their colors shifting and changing as the light hit them. I paused briefly at a booth where a woman painted people's dreams onto pressed leaves, her brushstrokes delicate and precise, each leaf a tiny, beautiful masterpiece.

It wasn't until I saw the table of preserved roots and enchanted seeds that I knew he was near. There was a certain hum that settled low in my chest when Aurelian was nearby—not a sound exactly, but more like a resonance, a feeling that seemed to vibrate within me. It was like the moment just before a bell is struck, when the air seems to hold its breath in anticipation. I followed it the way a dowsing rod follows water, letting it guide me through the crowded market.

And there he was. Leaning slightly over a display of spell-grown moss, his sleeves rolled up to his elbows, cheeks pink from the chill, and hair as wild as ever. He looked up the moment I stopped beside him, as if he had felt my presence just as I had felt his.

"Elowen," he said, my name rolling off his tongue like the start of a story he'd been waiting to read, a soft smile playing at the corners of his mouth.

"Lian," I replied, smiling before I could help it, his nickname feeling as natural on my lips as breathing.

"Whisker let you out unsupervised?" he asked, his eyes crinkling at the corners with amusement.

"Barely," I admitted with a laugh. "He warned me not to bring home more books. I think he's afraid they'll stage a coup and take over his favorite napping spots."

Aurelian grinned, a boyish charm that was impossible to resist. "Did you?" he asked, gesturing to my basket. "Bring home more books, that is."

"Probably," I confessed, returning his grin. It was no secret that I had a weakness for books, especially the old, rare, and magical variety. My bookshop was a testament to that, every nook and cranny filled with tomes that whispered stories of adventure, love, and enchantment.

He held up a tiny corked vial filled with glimmering, dust-colored seeds, their surfaces shimmering with an inner light. "These only bloom when someone tells the truth near them," he explained, his voice filled with a sense of wonder that was infectious.

"Oh," I said, amused by the idea. "Dangerous."

"I thought they might belong in your shop," he said, his eyes meeting mine. There was a sincerity in his gaze that made my heart flutter, as if we had known each other longer than the mere week that had passed since our first meeting. As if we were already something more than just acquaintances, something deeper and more meaningful.

"You didn't have to bring me anything," I protested softly, touched by the gesture.

"I didn't," he said simply, his voice filled with conviction. "They brought themselves to you."

I stared at the seeds for a long moment, their glimmering surfaces seeming to hold a world of possibilities. Then, slowly, I reached out and took the vial, our fingers brushing against each other, warm and ungloved. The market noise seemed to fade for a heartbeat, the world narrowing down to just the two of us, connected by the simplest of touches.

Then someone bumped into me from behind, the spell broken as suddenly as it had been cast. I tucked the seeds into my basket quickly, suddenly unsure of what to say, the moment too fragile for words.

"Have you eaten?" Aurelian asked, shifting the moment gently, his voice filled with concern.

"Not yet," I admitted, realizing that I had been so caught up in the magic of the market that I had forgotten about something as mundane as food.

"Then come with me," he said, his hand reaching out to guide me through the crowd, a promise of warmth and companionship in his touch.

We wound through the market together, the crowd parting around us like a river around a stone. We passed a stand with hand-dipped cinnamon candles, their sweet scent filling the air, and a booth where a tiny fae boy was trying to barter with enchanted marbles, his voice filled with determination as he haggled with the merchant. Aurelian stopped at the herb-roasted pie vendor, buying two small pastries filled with squash and leeks, their golden crusts glistening with melted butter. He handed one to me with a little napkin and a hopeful smile, his eyes watching my reaction carefully.

I took it and tried not to swoon as the flavors exploded on my tongue, the sweetness of the squash perfectly balanced by the savory leeks and the subtle hint of thyme. "This is criminally good," I murmured, my eyes closing briefly in appreciation.

"It's the thyme butter," he explained, his voice filled with pride. "A family recipe."

"You're spoiling me," I said between bites, the warmth of the pie spreading through me like a gentle embrace.

"Someone should," he said softly, his eyes meeting mine. There was a depth of feeling in his gaze that made my breath catch, a promise of something more than just friendship, something that whispered of shared dreams and whispered secrets.

I choked a little, not because of the food, but because of the sudden intensity of the moment, the realization that something had shifted between us, that we were standing on the precipice of something new and unknown.

He didn't laugh—just looked at me like he hadn't meant to say it aloud, but didn't regret it either. The leaves rustled high above us, their golden hues a stark contrast against the deep blue of the sky. One drifted down, caught by the breeze, and landed gently in my hair.

Aurelian reached for it slowly, his fingers brushing against my cheek as he removed the leaf, his touch lingering just a moment longer than necessary. Not enough to startle me, but just enough to feel real, to feel like a promise of things to come.

43

"You're glowing," he said softly, his voice filled with a sense of awe.

"It's the pie," I said, trying to deflect the compliment, my cheeks flushing with warmth.

He shook his head, his eyes never leaving mine. "It's you," he said simply, his voice filled with conviction.

I looked down, not because I was embarrassed, but because something in my chest was softening in ways I didn't have words for yet, a warmth that seemed to spread through me like the first rays of sunlight after a long, dark night. He didn't fill the silence, didn't try to force the moment, but simply walked beside me, his presence a comforting reassurance that I wasn't alone.

We spent another hour wandering the market, the sights and sounds a blur of color and noise around us. I bought a bundle of dried heather, its scent reminiscent of long summer days spent in the meadows outside of town. Aurelian picked up a spellbook of autumnal herbalism, its pages filled with riddles that hinted at ancient knowledge and hidden secrets. I caught him sneaking Whisker a treat at one booth, his eyes filled with mischief as he made me a promise it wasn't laced with pixie bark, a substance known for its unpredictable effects on both humans and animals alike.

The sun began to dip low over the rooftops, spilling gold across the cobbles, the light casting long shadows that seemed to dance and sway with a life of their own. The air grew cooler, the scent of woodsmoke and roasting chestnuts filling the air as the market prepared for the night ahead.

"I should get back," I said at last, reluctantly acknowledging the passage of time. "The bookshop gets restless when I'm gone too long."

"I'll walk you," Aurelian offered, without hesitation, his voice filled with a quiet determination.

And so we walked, side by side, as the lanterns overhead flickered to life, each one catching the last light of the sun and turning it into warmth, a beacon of hope and comfort in the gathering darkness. The market seemed to whisper around us, the voices of the merchants and the laughter of the children fading into the background, the world narrowing down to just the two of us, connected by something deeper than words, something that seemed to shimmer in the air between us like a promise of things to come.

45

When we reached my shop, Aurelian paused just outside the door, his hands tucked into his pockets, his eyes filled with a quiet intensity. Whisker stared at him through the window, his green eyes watching our every move like a judgmental chaperone, his tail flicking slowly behind him.

"Thank you," I said, unsure what I was thanking him for. The pie? The seeds? The way my name sounded softer when he said it, like a secret whispered between lovers?

He nodded once, a simple gesture that spoke volumes, his eyes never leaving mine. "Any time, Elowen," he said softly, the word a promise, a vow that seemed to hang in the air between us like a fragile, shimmering thread.

There it was again. That word. That promise. That sense of something more, something deeper, something that whispered of shared dreams and whispered secrets, of a future that was ours to shape, ours to claim.

I opened the door, letting the warm air and the scent of books wrap around me like a comforting embrace, a reminder of the world I knew, the world I loved. But as I stepped inside, I couldn't help but glance back, my eyes meeting Aurelian's one last time, a silent

46

acknowledgment of the moment we had shared, of the promise that hung in the air between us like a fragile, shimmering thread.

"See you tomorrow?" I asked, one foot already inside the shop, the other still lingering on the cobblestones, caught between the world I knew and the world that beckoned, a world filled with possibilities and promises, with dreams and desires that whispered in the shadows of my heart.

He smiled—not wide, not certain, but true, a smile that spoke of shared secrets and whispered dreams, of a future that was ours to shape, ours to claim.

"You always do," he said softly, his voice filled with conviction, a promise that seemed to shimmer in the air between us like a fragile, shimmering thread, a thread that connected us, that bound us, that whispered of a future that was ours to shape, ours to claim, ours to cherish, ours to love.

Chapter 6: A Cup Meant for Me

The first time she made me tea, I drank it too quickly. I didn't pause to savor it, didn't let the warmth linger on my tongue. I swallowed it down in hurried gulps, metal spoon clattering against the mug as I stirred absentmindedly.

It wasn't because the tea was hot, though steam curled from the surface in wispy tendrils, carrying with it a scent that promised comfort. And it wasn't because I was cold, though the chill of the day had seeped into my bones, making my fingers stiff and my breath visible in the crisp air.

I drank it quickly because I didn't trust what it made me feel. The warmth spreading through me wasn't just physical; it was something else, something more. A sensation I hadn't anticipated, one that caught me off guard and left me feeling exposed.

Comfort is dangerous when you don't expect it. It creeps up on you, silent and unseen, like the first light of dawn after a long, dark night. It disarms you, strips away your defenses one careful layer at a time. Softens your edges, smooths out the rough places you've come to rely on. Makes you look down at your hands, really look at them, and wonder how long they've been clenched tight, ready for a fight that never came.

She handed the tea to me without ceremony. No grand gestures or elaborate presentations. Just a simple mug, glazed in earthy tones, with a painted crescent moon on the side and a rim chipped from years of use. No spells whispered under her breath, no flourish of the hand. Just a quiet offering, plain and unadorned.

I think that's when I knew. That's when I understood that she saw things. Things that others didn't, things that maybe even I didn't want to see.

Not just in books, with their cracked spines and yellowed pages. But in people. In the lines etched into their faces, the stories hidden behind their eyes. She brewed that cup of tea like she'd already read the page I hadn't written yet, like she knew the tale I hadn't told.

Elowen doesn't ask questions the way others do. She doesn't poke and prod, doesn't pry open the locked places inside you. She makes room, creates space, and then she waits. Patiently, quietly, like the soil awaiting the first green shoots of spring.

And somehow, that's more intimate than anything else. More personal than any question she could have asked, any secret she could have demanded. She gives you the silence, the emptiness, and lets you fill it with whatever you choose.

That day in the shop—just after the festival, when the air was still thick with the scent of sweet pastries and smoke from the bonfires, just before the rain came and washed away the remnants of celebration—I watched her pour tea for an old villager. His hands shook as he told the same story three times, each iteration slightly different, slightly more frayed around the edges. She smiled at him each time like it was new, like she was hearing it for the first time. When he left, shuffling out into the gathering gloom, she didn't sigh or roll her eyes. She simply lit a candle, the flame flickering to life with a soft exhale of breath.

I didn't ask her why she did it. I didn't need to. The answer was there, in the gentle curve of her smile, the quiet strength of her hands as they cupped around the flame.

She tends to people the way she tends to her books. Carefully, with a deliberate slowness that seems almost reverent. Without hurrying them to be ready before they are, without rushing the process.

She understands that some things take time, that some stories can't be rushed.

I took my second cup slower. I let the heat of it seep into my palms, let the steam rise up and warm my face. She called it Hearthbrew, said it was for mending. For healing, for putting back together the pieces that had been broken.

I wondered if she meant me. If she saw the cracks and fissures that ran through me like fault lines, the places where I'd been shattered and put back together all wrong.

That day, I lingered long after the last sip was gone. I pretended I was reading the runes carved into the wall lantern, tracing their shapes with my fingertips as if deciphering some ancient code. But the truth was, I didn't want to leave. Not the tea, not the warmth it had spread through me.

Her.

When I got back to the grove quarters that night, the wind howling outside my window like a wild beast, I wrote down a single line in my journal. The words came unbidden, flowing from my pen as if they'd been waiting there all along.

"I think she's brewing something in me."

51

And for the first time in seasons, I didn't feel the need to leave in the morning. I didn't wake with that familiar itch in my feet, that restless urge to move on, to keep going. Instead, I felt something different. Something new.

I felt the need to return. To go back to that little shop, with its dusty books and chipped mugs and quiet understanding. To her.

Chapter 7: Rootbound

The morning's first light was barely a whisper when the bell above the door chimed tentatively, its voice echoing through the quiet shop like a hesitant visitor, unsure of its welcome. The tea leaves were still steeping in the pot, their aroma slowly unfurling into the air, when I heard the soft jingle.

I knew who it was even before I turned around. There was only one person who would come by this early, who would walk through the mist-laden streets with a secret cradled in his arms like a precious offering.

Aurelian stood in the doorway, his hair dampened by the morning's breath, his coat slightly askew as if he had hurried here without a thought for his appearance. He held something carefully wrapped in muslin, his arms curved protectively around it. He looked like he had stepped out of a dream, carrying a fragment of it with him into the waking world.

"I know it's early," he said, his voice quick and soft, "but I couldn't sleep. My mind was restless, and my feet led me here."

"You don't need an excuse," I replied, setting aside the tea strainer. "The shop is always awake, always ready for those who seek its comfort."

He stepped inside, brushing off a few stubborn chestnut leaves that clung to his boots. Whisker, perched on the poetry shelf, blinked once in his languid way and didn't move. That was his version of approval, a silent welcome to the familiar figure who had entered his domain.

Aurelian held out the bundle to me, his hands steady and sure. "I found this last night, tucked away in the folds of a hollowed root at the edge of the Moonwood. I think it's a fragment of an old ritual. Seasonal magic, perhaps."

I took the bundle carefully, feeling the cool, slightly damp cloth in my hands. Inside were brittle pages, their ink faded and edges ringed with pressed ferns. Beneath the parchment lay a root, split cleanly down the middle, as if it had once been part of something larger, something whole.

My breath caught in my throat as I realized the age of the artifact. "This is old," I murmured, more to myself than to him.

"Older than either of us," Aurelian agreed, his voice low. "But it called to me. And I thought... if anyone could help piece it back together, it would be you."

My fingers brushed one of the pages, and a soft pulse of warmth echoed back, as if the magic within was stirring, awakening from a long slumber. It was the kind of magic that slept until it was remembered, until it was needed once more.

"I'll need time," I said, looking up at him.

He smiled, holding out a jar labeled *Rootwake Blend*. "I brought tea," he said, as if that was the most natural thing in the world. As if he knew that the path to understanding the past was paved with patience and steeped in shared silences.

So we worked.

The back room filled with the scent of earth and parchment, the aroma of ancient words and forgotten rituals mingling with the smell of freshly brewed tea. We laid the fragments out on the long table, each one weighted with smooth stones and dried fruit slices to flatten the edges, to coax them back into their original form. Aurelian scribbled translation notes in his neat, precise handwriting, while I gently reapplied tracing charms to the nearly vanished runes, my fingers moving with a practiced ease.

It wasn't glamorous work. There was no flash of magic, no dramatic incantations. Just the steady rhythm of thought and breath, of brushing ink into faded grooves, of reading aloud the names of plants that no longer grew anywhere but in memory. It felt like breathing in harmony, our hearts beating in time with the pulse of the ancient magic that surrounded us.

"Did you always want to be a bookseller?" Aurelian asked quietly, his voice barely above a whisper, as if he was afraid to disturb the delicate balance of the moment.

I paused, quill poised above the parchment. "No," I admitted, a small smile playing on my lips. "I wanted to be a lantern maker."

He blinked, surprise etched on his features. "Truly?"

I nodded, my smile widening. "When I was young, I thought the fae who made the lanterns at the Autumn Market were the most powerful beings in the world. They created light that made people feel things—joy, sorrow, wonder. I wanted that. To make things that glowed, that cast light into the darkest corners of the heart."

"And now?" he asked, his voice soft, his eyes searching.

"I make books glow," I said, tapping the corner of one page where the ink had begun to shimmer faintly, like the first light of dawn breaking through the night. "A different kind of lantern, perhaps, but one that casts a light just as powerful."

He was quiet for a moment, his gaze thoughtful. Then, softly, he asked, "What happened to your father?"

The question came gently, with no push, no pry. Just an offering of space, an invitation to share the burden of the past.

I set down the quill, my hands suddenly heavy with the weight of memory.

"He was a traveling scholar," I began, my voice steady despite the ache in my heart. "Always chasing stories, always seeking the next tale to tell. One autumn, he left for a research trip into the west woods. Said he'd be back before the equinox."

Aurelian didn't speak. He didn't need to. The silence between us was filled with understanding, with shared sorrow.

"He never came back," I finished, my voice barely above a whisper. "And no one could find him. Not even the Seekers, with all their magic and their knowledge of the woods."

57

Aurelian's gaze never left mine, his eyes filled with a warmth that was both comforting and disconcerting. "I'm sorry," he said, his voice soft, his words a gentle caress against the raw edges of my grief.

"He left me this place," I said, waving vaguely to the shelves around us, to the books that held the echoes of his laughter, the remnants of his dreams. "And a habit of falling in love with forgotten things."

The room was quiet again, the air filled with the weight of shared truths, of old sorrows and new understandings.

And then, as if summoned by the weight of truth, Whisker leapt onto the table, right into our careful arrangement, his tail flicking with a mischievous gleam in his eyes. He knocked over the tiny vial of truth-telling seeds, the cork popping loose and the seeds scattering like stardust across the parchment and floor, glimmering faintly in the air as they landed.

"Oh no—" I began, my voice singing with exasperation.

"Whisker," I hissed, reaching out to scoop up the scattered seeds. "You absolute gremlin."

But Aurelian laughed, his eyes crinkling at the corners, his laughter a warm, infectious sound that filled the room with a sudden, unexpected light. "He has impeccable timing," he said, his voice filled with amusement.

The seeds reacted instantly to the energy in the room, glowing more brightly when either of us spoke, even when no sound passed our lips. They were like tiny beacons of truth, illuminating the path between us, guiding us towards a deeper understanding of each other.

I looked down at them, glowing soft gold where they had fallen near Aurelian's hand.

He traced a fingertip along the grain of the table, his voice barely above a whisper as he said, "I never felt like I belonged anywhere until I stepped into your shop."

My breath caught in my throat, his words striking a chord deep within me.

He didn't look at me when he said it. He didn't need to. The words weren't for performance. They were for the space between us, for the quiet, sacred ground where our hearts met.

I didn't know how to answer. I didn't know how to put into words the feelings that were stirring within me, the emotions that were rising like a tide, threatening to sweep me away.

So I reached across the table and offered him my hand.

59

He took it, his hand warm and calloused, steady and sure. Not possessive. Not demanding. Just... there. With mine.

The seeds glowed brighter, their light a silent testimony to the truth that passed between us, to the connection that was growing, like a tender shoot breaking through the earth, reaching towards the sun.

Later, after we'd cleaned up the seeds and restored what we could of the ritual, Aurelian stood at the door, readying to leave. The afternoon light cast a warm glow on his features, highlighting the lines of his face, the soft curve of his lips.

"I'll keep working on the translation," he said, his voice steady, his eyes intent.

"I'll be here," I replied, a small smile playing on my lips. "I always am."

But as he stepped outside, I noticed something odd. The lantern above the door—one of the market-made ones I'd hung just for the season—was burning brighter than it had the night before. Almost as if someone had whispered a secret into it, breathing life into its flame, making it glow with a newfound intensity.

"Aurelian," I called, my voice soft but clear, carrying through the stillness of the afternoon.

He turned, hand resting on the railing, his eyes searching mine.

"That lantern wasn't glowing like that this morning," I said, my gaze fixed on the bright light that seemed to defy the fading day.

He followed my gaze, his eyes lingering on the lantern before turning back to me. "Must be the magic," he said, a small smile playing on his lips.

"From the seeds?" I asked, my voice filled with wonder.

"From the moment," he replied, his voice soft, his words a gentle caress against the soft silence of the afternoon.

I watched him walk away until he disappeared into the copper-colored fog, his figure swallowed by the mists that clung to the edges of the day. And for the first time in a long while, I didn't feel like I was waiting for anything. I was simply here. And so was he. And in that moment, that was enough. That was everything.

Chapter 8: The Memory Jar

Some days drift into existence with a hushed sigh, barely stirring the air. No storms or sunbursts to herald their arrival. No festivals or bells declaring their purpose. Just the quiet hum of life, the ticking of the clock, and the gentle beat of a heart waiting for something undefined, something yet to be named.

That was the sort of morning that greeted me. The world outside was draped in a thick fog, the kind that muffles sounds and blurs the edges of everything it touches. Faerrow was shrouded in this gentle haze, its buildings and people softened, their sharp corners rounded and muted.

The shop was bathed in a stillness that seemed to slow time itself. I struck a match and touched it to the wick of a single candle on the front counter—vanilla and sage, its scent familiar and comforting. I let it burn slow and steady as I settled into the window seat, a cup of tea warming my hands. Whisker was curled beside me like a sentient comma, his purrs a soft metronome against the quiet.

A few regulars trickled in and out—Mirren the weaver, her fingers stained with dye, seeking tales of river-spirits to inspire her latest tapestry. Old Thom, his gnarled hands clutching a worn copy of the fae crossword book, needing a replacement because he'd spilled cider on the last one. These small, rhythmic interactions were the pulse of my life, giving it shape and cadence.

But all morning, something felt... different. An undercurrent of expectation hummed beneath the surface, like the shop itself was holding its breath.

I didn't understand why until I opened the drawer behind the counter and found it again.

A memory jar.

It was small—a glass vessel no taller than my palm, sealed with wax and a single faded ribbon that had once been a vibrant red. Inside the jar holds a slip of parchment, a season-old memory I'd written and sealed inside. It had been my mother's tradition before it became mine: every week in autumn, you write down a memory that still lingers, still aches or hums, and hide it in a jar. On the last night of the season, you read them all by candlelight and decide which to keep... and which to let go.

63

I hadn't added anything in years.

Not until today.

The page I tore was cream-colored, faintly textured, like it belonged in a book about beginnings. I wrote:

The way his fingers brushed mine over the root-fragment, sending a spark dancing across my skin. The way my name sounded softer when he said it, like a secret whispered into the wind. The way I wanted him to say it again, to feel that warmth unfurl within me once more.

I folded it gently, sealed it with wax, and slipped it inside a jar.

The moment I did, the air in the shop shifted—just slightly. Like the books had leaned in to listen, their spines creaking softly in anticipation.

Whisker raised his head, his ears pricked forward.

"What?" I asked him, my voice barely above a whisper. "I'm allowed to feel things, you know."

He blinked slowly, then leapt off the window seat as the front bell chimed, its melodic ring echoing through the shop.

I didn't even need to look up. I knew who it was.

Aurelian stepped inside, his cheeks flushed from the brisk walk, a linen-wrapped bundle tucked under one arm. His eyes met mine, and he smiled, a warm curve of his lips that made something flutter in my chest.

"I brought pumpkin bread," he said, by way of greeting, setting the bundle on the counter. He pulled a thermos from his satchel, its metal surface catching the glow of the candlelight. "And rosehip tea to balance the sweetness."

I smiled back, feeling a warmth spread through me that had nothing to do with the tea. "Still trying to bribe your way into the shop's good graces?"

"I'm trying to bribe you," he said, his voice low and earnest. "And I brought enough for sharing."

"You've thought this through," I said, raising an eyebrow but unable to keep the amusement from my voice.

"I've been thinking," he admitted, his gaze steady on mine. There was something in his voice, an undercurrent of seriousness that made me pause.

He held my gaze, unwavering. "Can we sit for a while? Just... without ink or tasks?"

65

I nodded once, slowly. "Of course."

We settled in the window seat, the cushions dipping beneath our weight. Whisker took the high ground on the shelf above us, his tail swishing lazily like a self-appointed guardian. Aurelian poured the tea, its floral warmth curling between us like a living thing, a tendril of steam reaching out to touch my face. The bread was soft and spiced, the kind that crumbles gently in your hands, leaving traces of cinnamon and nutmeg on your fingertips.

Neither of us spoke for a long time. And it wasn't awkward. It was... comfortable. Honest. The kind of silence that doesn't need filling, that speaks volumes in its quietude.

Eventually, he said, "Do you ever worry that places can forget you?"

I blinked, taken aback by the question. "What do you mean?"

He stared at the rising steam, his eyes tracing its path as it dissipated into the air. "I've been gone from Faerrow so long. I wondered, when I returned, if it would remember me. If I'd feel like I belonged."

"You do," I said, the words slipping out before I could think them through. Then, softer, "I think the place remembers kindness. Stillness. Roots."

His eyes flicked to me, their depths filled with something unspoken. "Then maybe that's why I found you."

I looked down quickly, but not before I saw the way he softened when he said it. I picked at the edge of my mug, my fingers tracing the small chip in the glaze. "I found a memory jar this morning," I said, my voice barely above a whisper.

"Oh?" He leaned in slightly, his interest piqued.

"It's an old tradition," I explained, my eyes still fixed on the mug. "You collect memories through the season. Seal them away until it's time to decide if they're meant to stay... or be let go."

"What did you write today?" he asked, his voice gentle, coaxing.

I hesitated, my heart pounding in my chest. "Just a few words. Something... soft."

He nodded, accepting that boundary with grace. "Would you show me sometime?"

"Maybe," I said, my voice barely audible. "If I decide to keep it."

He didn't ask what *it* was. But I think he knew.

As the sun dipped low, casting the world in a golden glow, Aurelian stood to leave. He gathered his satchel, tucking the thermos away with careful hands.

"Thank you," he said, his voice filled with sincerity. "For sitting with me. No rituals. No restoration. Just... here."

"I liked it," I said, watching his hands as they moved, their graceful dance mesmerizing. "I like when you're here."

The door creaked slightly as he opened it, the bell above chiming softly in farewell.

But before he left, he turned back, his hand still on the door. "Elowen?"

"Yes?" I looked up, my heart pounding in my chest.

"If I were a memory, would you keep me?"

I couldn't answer. The words lodged in my throat, held captive by the swell of emotions within me.

So I stepped forward, reached for the jar behind me, and pressed it into his hands.

68

"For safe keeping," I said, my voice steady despite the turmoil inside me.

His fingers closed around it with reverence, like he was holding something precious, something fragile.

"I'll guard it with everything," he said, his voice filled with promise.

And then he was gone, the lantern above the door flickering like a breath held too long, then released. The shop seemed emptier without him, the air colder, the silence louder. But his words lingered, echoing in the stillness, wrapping around me like a warm embrace.

If I were a memory, would you keep me?

I didn't have an answer. Not yet. But perhaps, come the end of the season, when the last candle was lit and the final memory unfurled, I would. Perhaps then, I would know.

Chapter 9: The Path Between

Some days are meant for stillness, for the slow, steady rhythm of a quiet heart and a mind at peace. But I couldn't find it—not in the steaming cup of chamomile, not in the worn pages of familiar books, not even in the way Whisker watched me from the counter, his eyes narrowed and tail twitching like a metronome counting out the seconds of my disquiet.

The restlessness was a thrum under my skin, a ceaseless tide that ebbed and flowed with each breath. I looked at Whisker, his silhouette stark against the soft light filtering through the window. "You feel it too, don't you?" I asked, gently nudging his paw. He stretched languidly, giving a noncommittal yawn before jumping down from the counter and trotting toward the front door with an air of purpose.

That was all the answer I needed. I wrapped a woolen shawl around my shoulders, the one with the frayed edges and the faint scent of lavender, and grabbed Whisker's small bell-collar. The bell was enchanted, of course—he'd found a way to phase out of it twice, leaving nothing but empty leather and a silent chime. I fastened it securely and stepped out into the soft hush of Faerrow's late afternoon.

The fog had lifted, but the sky remained swathed in a blanket of clouds, holding onto the sun like a closely guarded secret. The streets were quieter than usual, the last remnants of the Lantern Market now packed away, leaving behind only faint traces of music that lingered like ghostly echoes and stray ribbons caught on lampposts, fluttering forlornly in the breeze.

Whisker led the way, his tail held high like a beacon, trotting along the cobblestone with an unerring sense of direction. He always did. His path was deliberate, as if he knew exactly where we needed to go, and I followed him, letting the familiar sights of Faerrow unfold around me.

We followed the edge of the square, past Mirren's weaving house with its windows filled with skeins of colored yarn, past the empty stone fountain where someone had left a cluster of fading sunflowers, their petals drooping like tired dancers after a long performance. I let myself meander, allowing the village to speak to me in its soft, subtle way. Faerrow never shouted; its magic whispered, a gentle breeze carrying secrets and stories through the air.

Some say that's why it was so hard to find unless it wanted you. The village had a will of its own, a sentient heart that beats in rhythm with the lives of its inhabitants. It reveals itself only to those who were meant to be here, who are drawn to its quiet magic like moths to a flame.

I paused beside the bridge at the far end of the square—the one that crossed a narrow stream just before the woods thickened into a dense tangle of trees and shadows. A flutter of movement caught my eye, and I knelt down, my skirts pooling around me on the damp grass. There, pressed against the edge of the railing like it had been caught in passing, was a small, flattened flower. A bell-shaped bloom, sky-blue with silver veins that shimmered in the waning light.

It pulsed faintly with residual magic, a soft, steady heartbeat that seemed to echo the rhythm of my own. I knew it wasn't from any garden in Faerrow. It was Aurelian's.

He used them as page markers—little living memories enchanted to preserve scent and shape, tiny fragments of time held captive within their delicate petals. I'd seen them when we worked on the ritual text together, his fingers brushing against mine as he turned the pages, the scent of the flowers mingling with the dusty smell of old parchment. He always pressed them between notes, almost absentmindedly, like someone tucking away thoughts he wasn't ready to say aloud.

I reached for it, my hand hovering in the air for a moment before I paused. Instead of plucking it free, I placed a finger gently on the petal, feeling the warmth and familiar hum of Aurelian's magic. It was a sensation I'd come to know well, a comforting presence that seemed to fill the room whenever he entered the shop, his eyes meeting mine with a soft, unspoken greeting.

Whisker meowed softly from ahead, his voice a plaintive call that broke through my reverie. I followed him down the footpath that circled behind the bookshop, a loop I usually only walked in autumn when the leaves turned golden and the air was crisp with the promise of change. Leaves crunched beneath my boots, and the trees above rustled with the sound of wind and whispers, the branches creaking like old bones as they swayed gently in the breeze.

I didn't know why I needed this walk until I was in the middle of it, the rhythm of my steps matching the steady beat of my heart.

73

Because something was shifting in me—a slow, inexorable movement, like the turning of the earth beneath my feet. And I was afraid to name it, afraid to give voice to the quiet longing that had taken root in the depths of my soul.

Aurelian hadn't made a move. Not one that pressed, not one that asked for anything more than the simple pleasure of my company. And yet, his presence felt like a vine slowly curling around something I hadn't realized was dormant, a root system reawakening after a long, cold winter. I'd spent so long building a quiet life for myself, a soft haven of books and spells and routines that didn't ask much of me beyond showing up, beyond being present in the stillness of each day.

But now, there were mornings I woke up hoping he'd come by before I finished my tea, the steam curling lazily in the air as I listened for the sound of his footsteps on the cobblestone path. There were nights I replayed the sound of him saying my name, the way his voice wrapped around the syllables like a caress, a gentle touch that lingered long after he'd gone.

And now, there were flowers pressed into the bones of the village, left behind like soft echoes of his presence, subtle reminders of the quiet magic that seemed to follow him wherever he went.

When I got back to *Thistle & Thread*, the sun had dipped behind the rooftops, casting long shadows across the square and turning the windows to gold. I stepped inside, brushing a leaf from Whisker's fur, and set the kettle to boil, the familiar ritual a comforting balm to my restless spirit.

I lit a candle at the counter—amber and fig, the scent filling the air with a warm, inviting glow—and reached for a blank card from the drawer. Another memory for the jar, another fragment of time captured in ink and paper, held safe against the ravages of forgetfulness.

I wrote, the words flowing from my pen like a secret, whispered into the quiet of the room:

A flower tucked into the railing, its petals a soft blue against the weathered wood. My name in his voice, a gentle caress that lingered long after he'd gone. A walk that wasn't aimless after all, but a journey toward something I couldn't yet name, a quiet longing that whispered in the rustle of the leaves and the soft hush of the wind.

I sealed the card, slipping it inside a jar where it joined the others, a collection of moments that told the story of my life in

Faerrow. The wax warmed beneath my fingers like a heartbeat, a steady pulse that seemed to echo the rhythm of my own.

I didn't know what tomorrow would bring. But I had a feeling I knew who would be waiting at the door, hair damp from the morning mist, tea in hand, and eyes full of something unspoken, a silent promise that hung in the air like the first light of dawn. And I wasn't afraid of that anymore. I was ready to step into the soft glow of tomorrow, to embrace the quiet magic that whispered in the wind and danced in the shadows, a gentle reminder of the life that awaited me, just beyond the edge of stillness.

Chapter 10: Heartbrew and Honeylight

The rain returned with no warning, as if the sky had been holding its breath all morning, waiting for the perfect moment to exhale. One moment, the clouds were merely brooding, hanging low and heavy, pregnant with vague promises. The next, the sky opened like a long-awaited sigh, pouring everything it had onto the rooftops of Faerrow. The raindrops chased each other down the cobblestone streets, drumming against the windows and doors with a sudden, insistent rhythm.

I stood at the window of *Thistle & Thread*, watching the drops paint intricate rivulets across the glass. The shop always felt cozier during storms, as if it gathered its breath and wrapped itself in a quilt of sound and shadow. The wind whispered secrets to the eaves, and the rain tapped out a soothing melody on the roof. The scent of old books and beeswax candles filled the air, a comforting blanket against the chill outside.

I didn't mind the solitude. In fact, I often welcomed it, cherishing the quiet moments when the shop was empty, and the books seemed to hum softly to themselves. But today, I found myself glancing at the door more often than I cared to admit, my eyes flicking up from the pages of my book, anticipating the familiar jingle of the bell.

Whisker was curled up in the window seat, his paws tucked neatly under his chin. His tail twitched lazily, the only sign of life aside from the slow rise and fall of his chest. The storm didn't bother him in the slightest; he was content to watch the rain with half-closed eyes, as if it were a performance put on for his benefit alone.

"Do you think he'll come today?" I asked softly, my voice barely audible over the patter of the rain. I wasn't sure why I was asking Whisker; he couldn't understand me, of course. But sometimes, it helped to say the words aloud, to give voice to the thoughts that circled endlessly in my mind.

Whisker blinked slowly, then flicked an ear, as if to say, "Why wouldn't he?" I took that as a yes, a small smile tugging at the corners of my mouth.

The kettle began to whistle just as the bell above the door jingled, its cheerful chime cutting through the shop's hushed atmosphere. I turned, already smiling, already knowing who I would find standing there.

Aurelian stood in the doorway, rain-drenched and golden at the edges—like a story walking in from a page someone had left open too long. His coat was soaked through, his curls dripping onto his shoulders, and his cheeks were flushed with cold and something more. Something that made my heart beat a little faster, my breath catch in my throat.

"I brought thyme bread," he said, holding up a small paper-wrapped parcel. His voice was warm, a soft rumble that seemed to fill the room, chasing away the chill that had settled in the corners.

"I'll make tea," I replied, my heart warming before my hands even reached the cups. I turned away from him, busying myself with the kettle and the tea leaves, trying to ignore the flutter in my chest.

The scent of Heartbrew filled the room as we settled into the reading nook, Whisker reluctantly making room for Aurelian on the rug. The fire in the hearth snapped softly, casting golden light across the shelves and our clasped mugs. The rain continued to tap against the window, but the sound was softer here, muted by the thick walls and the cozy warmth of the shop.

79

"You always bring the weather with you," I teased, trying to ignore the way my heart pounded in my chest.

"I was hoping for fog," he said, his voice low and warm. "But I'll settle for you."

I pretended to focus on pouring the tea, though I could feel the words bloom warm across my collarbones, could feel the heat rising in my cheeks. I handed him his cup, our fingers brushing briefly, and tried to ignore the spark that passed between us.

I watched him cradle his cup, steam curling between his fingers like breath. There was something so intimate about the gesture, something that made me feel as if I were intruding on a private moment. But he didn't seem to mind my gaze; instead, he looked up at me, his eyes reflecting the firelight, and smiled.

He took a slow sip, then sighed, a soft, contented sound that seemed to resonate deep within me. "This one tastes like memory. And quiet things. Safe things."

"It's called Heartbrew," I told him, my voice barely above a whisper. "It knows when something needs mending."

Aurelian leaned back, watching the rain trace trails down the window. "It's easier to breathe here," he said, his voice barely audible.
80

"As if the very air is different, somehow. As if it's filled with stories and dreams and all the things that make life worth living."

I looked at him, my heart thudding softly in my chest. "That's what I wanted when I reopened this place after my father," I said, my voice barely above a whisper. "Not just a bookshop. A space that... remembers. A space that holds onto the stories and the dreams and the magic that so often get lost in the rush of everyday life."

He didn't speak right away, but when he did, it was softer than the fire, softer than the rain against the window. "You made something sacred," he said, his eyes never leaving mine. "A sanctuary, a refuge. A place where people can come to remember who they are, and who they want to be."

We drank in companionable silence, the kind that fills a room rather than empties it. The shop held its breath around us, as if even the magic didn't want to interrupt. The fire crackled softly, and the rain continued to tap against the window, but the world outside seemed distant, somehow—as if we were suspended in a moment out of time, a pocket of warmth and light in the midst of the storm.

Whisker sprawled across Aurelian's lap with a dramatic thump, his eyes closing the instant Aurelian's hand found the right

81

rhythm behind his ears. I raised an eyebrow, a small smile playing at the corners of my mouth. "He hasn't liked anyone since Midsummer," I said, my voice barely above a whisper.

"Then perhaps he's been waiting for me," Aurelian said, not missing a beat. His eyes met mine, steady and sure, and I felt something shift within me, something that had been waiting, like Whisker, for the right moment to reveal itself.

I tilted my head, studying him, trying to read the thoughts that flickered behind his eyes. "You really believe that?" I asked, my voice soft, barely audible over the crackle of the fire.

"I don't think Whisker settles for less than destiny," he said, his voice steady, his gaze never wavering from mine.

I laughed—quietly, but truly, the sound bubbling up from deep within me, a wellspring of joy I hadn't known was there. "That's a lot of pressure," I said, my voice barely above a whisper.

He looked at me then—not past me, not through me, but *at* me. And in that moment, I forgot what it felt like to carry everything alone. I forgot the weight of the shop, the weight of the stories and the dreams and the magic that filled its shelves. I forgot everything except the

82

warmth of his gaze, the steady beat of my heart, and the knowledge that, in this moment at least, I was not alone.

"Elowen," he said, my name softer than rain, softer than the firelight that danced across his features. "Do you ever wonder what your magic would look like to someone else?"

I blinked, surprised by the question. "No one's ever asked me that," I said, my voice barely above a whisper. I had always known that my magic was different, that it was tied to the shop and the stories it contained. But I had never thought about what it might look like to someone else, how it might manifest in the eyes of another.

"I think it would look like this," he said, gesturing to the shelves, the fire, the way the shadows curved around us gently. "Like warmth you didn't know you were missing. Like something whole."

And before I could say something that would ruin it, I leaned in, just a little, and said the only thing I could manage.

"Lian."

His eyes met mine, focused, steady. "You say that like you've known my name forever," he said, his voice barely above a whisper.

"Maybe I have," I whispered, my heart pounding in my chest. "Maybe I just needed a reason to say it."

The fire popped once, a soft, comforting sound that seemed to echo the beat of my heart. Whisker purred louder, his contentment a tangible thing, a warmth that seemed to radiate out from his furry body and envelop us both.

And then I added, quieter still, "Leafheart."

He laughed then smiled that soft, rare smile he gives only in stillness, only in moments like this, when the world seemed to hold its breath around us.

The tea went cold. The rain slowed, its frenzied pace giving way to a gentle patter that seemed to lull the world to sleep. But neither of us moved. We stayed in that pocket of time, that in-between space the world forgot, where nothing needed to be decided, and everything already was.

And for once, I didn't write it down for the jar. I didn't try to capture the moment, to hold onto it with words and ink and paper. Instead, I kept it in me, a warmth that spread from my heart outward, a memory that would sustain me through the coldest nights and the darkest days. A memory that would remind me, always, that I was not alone, that there was magic in the world, and that sometimes, just sometimes, it found its way to me.

Chapter 11: The Seed Grows Quietly

She says my name like it is part of the shop, as if it was woven into the very fabric of the place. Like it had always lived in the walls, echoing softly through the peeling plaster and the faded paint. It was there in the dust between the shelves, clinging to the aged spines of books and the worn edges of antique trinkets. It drifted in the steam of the tea she brewed without measuring, the aroma of which filled the air like an old, familiar song.

"Lian."

Soft. Unafraid. The sound of it was as gentle as the first light of dawn, yet it held a strength that belied its quietude. It wasn't a nickname—not really. It was more a discovery, as if she'd plucked something invisible from the air and held it up, recognizing it as already mine. As if she'd found a piece of me that I hadn't even known was missing.

And the worst part? I wanted to hear it again. I still do. There's a longing within me, a hunger that gnaws at my heart, urging me to return to that moment, to that place, to hear her speak my name once more.

That night, after the Heartbrew had cooled and the rain had softened to a mist against the windowglass, I didn't want to leave. It wasn't because I was tired or weary from the day. It was because, for the first time in what felt like an eternity, I finally felt like I belonged. I belonged to a moment that didn't need explaining, a moment that simply was, pure and unadulterated.

The way she looked at me—it was as if I was already part of the room's design, as if I'd always been there, a fixture as permanent as the ancient beams overhead or the worn floorboards beneath our feet. There was no judgment in her gaze, no question or expectation. Just acceptance, warm and unyielding.

The way Whisker didn't protest when I shifted, his small body leaning into my touch as if it were the most natural thing in the world. He purred softly, the sound a comforting rhythm that filled the silence but did not shatter it.

For the silence wasn't empty. It was alive, a living, breathing thing that wrapped around us, cocooning us in its peaceful embrace.

It was a silence that told stories, that whispered secrets in the language of the heart.

There's a kind of magic in Faerrow that doesn't announce itself with fanfare or spectacle. It doesn't burst from stones or hover above fields in a blaze of glory. No, it lingers. It settles in the quiet places, the in-between spaces, waiting patiently for permission to be seen, to be felt.

Elowen is like that. She's magic, pure and simple, but she doesn't flaunt it. She doesn't need to. It's there in her eyes, in her smile, in the way she moves through the world with a grace that seems almost otherworldly.

When she called me Leafheart—half teasing, half something else, something deeper and more profound—I laughed. But even as the laughter bubbled up from within me, I felt it. I felt her reach into the soil of my chest and tug on something growing there. Something I hadn't planted, something I hadn't even known existed until that very moment. But she saw it. She saw me. And she was watering it anyway, nurturing it with her kindness, her acceptance, her love.

When I left that evening, I didn't go straight home. I couldn't. Not yet. I walked to the edge of the grove, past the memory bulbs with their soft, ethereal glow and the rootlines that snaked across the ground like veins. I sat on a stone worn smooth by time and wind, the surface cool and comforting beneath me.

I didn't write anything down. Not in my journal, the pages of which remained blank and untouched. Not in the soil, the secrets of which stayed buried and hidden from view. But I pressed my palm to the ground, feeling the heartbeat of the earth pulsing beneath my touch. And I whispered the name she gave me.

Leafheart.

And for the first time in years, the ground whispered something back. A secret, a promise, a truth that resonated deep within my soul. A truth that told me I was home.

Chapter 12: Inkroot and Echoes

There was a soft, almost tentative knock at the back door. Not the front, where strangers and casual acquaintances would typically announce their arrival, and not the bell, which would have echoed through the house with an impersonal chime. Just two gentle taps, followed by a slight pause, then one more—a rhythm that was familiar in the way old melodies are, stirring something within me that was more feeling than thought. I recognized it not for what it signified, but for whom it announced.

I looked down at my ink-stained fingers, the remnants of a day spent lost in words and illustrations. Wiping them clean with a well-worn cloth, I made my way to the door, feeling a quiet anticipation build within me. As I opened it, Aurelian stood on the other side, his expression bearing that not-quite-smile that always seemed to hold a world of unspoken words. It was like the first line of a favorite poem, inviting you to step into its rhythm and lose yourself in its story. His coat, for once, was dry, draped neatly over his arm despite the day's earlier rain. He held a bundle, carefully wrapped in cloth, about the size of a shoebox.

"Don't say anything yet, I found something else in the grove," he said, his eyes gleaming with an excitement that was almost contagious. "Just let me show you."

I stepped aside, my heart already flickering with curiosity and something more—something that felt like the first embers of a long-dormant fire.

We moved into the restoration room, the air still carrying the faint scent of rosehip and ash from the tea we had shared the day before. The room was filled with the soft, warm light of late afternoon, casting long shadows that danced gently with the slightest draft. I cleared a space on the large wooden table that dominated the center of the room, pushing aside half-finished projects, stacks of parchment, and the other found book I was restoring, to make way for whatever treasure Aurelian had brought.

He set the bundle down with a reverence that was almost sacred, his hands careful and deliberate as he began to unwrap it layer by layer. Inside was an another book—or at least, what remained of one. The cover was stitched from pressed bark, its texture rough and

90

uneven, bearing the marks of time and weather. The pages were scattered, their edges uneven and frayed, bound only by a single black root that pulsed faintly with a magic that seemed to hum softly, as if remembering the touch of hands long past.

"Inkroot," Aurelian said quietly, his voice barely above a whisper, as if speaking too loudly might disturb the delicate balance of the book's magic. "It's rare. I found it tangled in a northern grove, hidden among the roots of ancient trees. The pages were whispering, calling out to be heard."

I reached out, my fingers hovering over the edge of one of the pages before lightly touching it. A faint tingling sensation ran through my fingertips, like the first tendrils of a spell taking hold.

"They're still connected," I said, my voice filled with wonder.

"Even though they've scattered," he replied, meeting my eyes with a look that held more than just shared knowledge—it held understanding, a silent acknowledgment of the metaphor that neither of us needed to voice.

The next hour passed in a quiet collaboration, the kind that feels as natural as breathing. We sorted the pages by feel more than logic, our hands moving in a dance that seemed guided by something deeper than thought. The ink on the pages shimmered faintly when we guessed right, glowing just enough to encourage us, to let us know we were on the right path. We didn't rush. Magic like this didn't want to be hurried—it wanted company, intention, breath. It wanted to be coaxed gently into being, like a shy creature emerging from its hiding place.

Aurelian's sleeve brushed mine more than once as we worked, the soft fabric of his shirt whispering against my skin. Neither of us pulled away. Instead, we let the moment linger, the space between us filled with the unspoken words of a conversation that didn't need to be voiced.

"Some of these symbols are pre-Faerrow," I said, squinting at a line of looped script that seemed to shift and change with each passing moment. "Your mossy archive friends would weep with joy if they saw this."

"They'd also try to lock it up," he replied, a hint of a smile playing at the corners of his mouth. "That's why I brought it to you."

"To hide it?" I asked, looking up from the page to meet his gaze.

"To heal it," he said, his voice soft but firm, filled with a conviction that sent a shiver down my spine.

I stilled, my hands pausing in their work. "That's not something I know how to do," I said, the words feeling like a confession, a secret whispered into the quiet of the room.

"Yes," he said, meeting my eyes with a look that held no room for doubt, "it is."

We paused as the candles burned lower, the light dipping into a warm amber that matched the hush between our breaths. The room seemed to hold its breath with us, the shadows growing longer and softer, like the gentle fingers of twilight reaching out to touch the edges of our world. Whisker had long since made a nest for himself behind the jars of dried herbs that lined the shelf, his gentle snores filling the room with a comforting rhythm.

Aurelian picked up one of the half-bound pages, holding it up to the light as if trying to read the secrets hidden within its faded ink. He spoke almost to himself, his voice barely above a whisper, "There's something about sitting across from you that makes me want to remember things I didn't know I'd forgotten."

93

My throat tightened, the words wrapping around my heart like the roots of the inkroot book, binding me to this moment, to this man.

I looked down, tracing the lines of the root where it wound through the binding, my fingers following its path as if it were a road map to a place I'd long forgotten. "Like what?" I asked, the words barely audible, as if speaking them too loudly might break the delicate spell that held us in its thrall.

"Like how good silence can feel," he said, his voice filled with a quiet wonder, as if he were discovering this truth for the first time. "Like how warmth isn't always fire."

I didn't answer. Instead, I reached across the table, toward the fragile center of the book, and placed my hand over his. The root glowed where we touched it, its light pulsing gently, like the beat of a heart long thought lost.

And then, impossibly, it grew—just a sliver, just enough to bridge the space between the two last unconnected pages. It was a small thing, barely noticeable, but it felt like a promise, a whispered secret shared between the three of us—Aurelian, the book, and me.

He looked at me then, and I realized he'd known all along. That this wasn't just about a book. It was about something root-deep, something that chose to grow here, with both of us, in the quiet spaces between our breaths and the soft light of the setting sun.

Later, after he'd gone—after he'd paused in the doorway, taken my hand in his, and pressed a soft kiss to the back of it without asking, without needing to ask—I sat with the newly restored pages and felt their hum settle into the shelves, their magic becoming a part of the room, a part of me. I thought about the jar on the counter, the one filled with the memories I'd sealed inside it, each one a moment captured and preserved, like a flower pressed between the pages of a book.

I didn't write one tonight. Some moments don't belong on paper. Some just need to be planted and trusted to grow, to become a part of the story that weaves itself through our lives, connecting us to the people and the places that make us who we are. And as I sat there, in the quiet of the restoration room, with the hum of the inkroot book filling the air, I knew that this was one of those moments—a memory not to be captured, but to be lived, to be breathed, to be allowed to grow and change and become something more. Something root-deep, something true.

Chapter 13: Moonlight and Memoryleaf

That night, sleep was an elusive creature, dancing just out of reach. It wasn't the kind of restlessness that stemmed from worry or discomfort, but rather a stirring from deep within—a quiet, insistent blossoming that demanded my attention, like a flower unfurling its petals under the moonlight.

In the silence of my room, I struck a match, the sound of it igniting a sharp contrast to the night's hush. I lit a candle, not one of the ordinary ones from the shop stock, but a personal treasure plucked from my private shelf. It was crafted from golden beeswax, infused with crushed lavender that released a soothing fragrance as it warmed. Laced within was a subtle hint of memoryleaf—the kind of candle that burned with a clarity that was almost too bright, leaving one wide awake, with a heart softened and thoughts amplified beyond their usual bounds, stretching out like shadows in the candlelight.

Whisker followed me downstairs without so much as a whisper, his tail brushing against the stairs like a silk ribbon, a comforting presence in the quietude of the night. I didn't bother with the lights; the moonlight streaming through the windows was more than sufficient, casting a silver glow over everything it touched, transforming the familiar into something almost ethereal.

I prepared the tea meticulously, following the method my mother had taught me years ago—by feel and intuition, not by precise measurement. Moonlight tea wasn't meant for casual sipping; it was a brew for remembrance, for stirring the depths of the soul. I added a pinch of jasmine for clarity of thought, watching as the tiny flowers floated in the pot, releasing their delicate scent. Then, two dried rose petals for a touch of tenderness, their softness a gentle reminder of love's presence. A curl of memoryleaf was next, for the words I was too cautious to utter aloud, the leaves unfurling in the hot water like secrets waiting to be told. Finally, the faintest shimmer of crushed starlace—just enough to catch the light, but not enough to be considered truly magical, a hint of sparkle in the night.

I poured the hot water over the mixture and let it steep, allowing the aroma to fill the room, a comforting scent that wrapped around me like a warm embrace. Outside, the village lay hushed, blanketed in a silver sheen under the moon's watchful gaze. Every rooftop and window gleamed as if touched by something sacred, a silent testament to the night's tranquility, a world held in a peaceful slumber.

I didn't expect the knock at the door, but when it came, I wasn't surprised. It was as if the night itself had whispered his arrival. I opened the door before he had a chance to knock a second time, the cool night air brushing against my skin. Aurelian stood in the lamplight, his hair tousled from the night breeze, sleeves pushed up to his elbows, his breath caught in a quiet, steady rhythm. He didn't speak immediately, as if gathering his thoughts or perhaps his courage, his eyes reflecting the soft glow of the candlelight.

"You felt it too," I said softly, breaking the silence that hung between us like a delicate veil.

He nodded, a slight movement in the dim light, an acknowledgment that needed no words. "Couldn't sleep," he said, his voice a low murmur that blended with the night's hush.

I stepped aside, inviting him into the shop. He entered as if he already belonged there, his presence fitting naturally into the space, as if the room itself welcomed him. We settled onto the rug in front of the fireplace, though no flames danced within. The room was lit only by the glow of the candle and the lingering warmth of the floor, still clinging to the memory of the day's sun, a soft embrace that enveloped us.

I handed him the second mug without a word, and he took it carefully, his eyes flicking to mine with a questioning glance, as if seeking confirmation of the unspoken understanding between us.

"Moonlight tea?" he asked, his voice barely above a whisper, a gentle inquiry that hung in the air like a soft melody.

"Memoryleaf," I replied softly, the word a secret shared between us, a key to the night's mysteries.

He smiled, a gentle curve of his lips that held a world of unspoken emotions. "Of course," he said, the words a soft sigh that blended with the night's peace.

The tea was still too warm to drink, so he cradled the cup in his hands, leaning back against the bookshelf. I found myself watching the way his fingers moved over the ceramic, as if they held secrets, as if they remembered things I was still learning to grasp, a dance of shadows and light that told a story only we could understand.

"Elowen," he said, not looking at me directly, his gaze fixed on some distant point, as if seeing beyond the walls of the room, beyond the boundaries of the night. "Can I tell you something without asking for anything in return?"

My heart fluttered in my chest, a gentle wingbeat of anticipation, a whisper of excitement that echoed through me. "Yes," I whispered, the word a soft breath that hung in the air between us.

"I've never stayed in one place long enough to want anything permanent," he began, his voice steady yet laced with a hint of vulnerability, a confession that held the weight of a thousand unsaid words. "But I think I'm starting to understand what roots feel like."

I looked at him, truly looked at him, and saw it—the flicker of fear in his honesty, the bravery in the choice to say it anyway, a strength that shone like a beacon in the night. And I didn't respond with words. Instead, I shifted closer, our knees touching just barely, a connection that held a world of meaning. I reached out and placed my hand over his on the mug, the warmth passing between us like a shared secret, a bond that transcended the boundaries of time and space.

The tea shimmered, not from the heat, but from the magic that exists in the space between silence and confession, a dance of light and shadow that told a story of its own. He looked at me then, really looked. And for one breathless moment, the distance between us was gone. Not a kiss, but a closeness that was almost more intimate. Foreheads nearly touching, his hand in mine, my name in his breath, a moment suspended in time, a fragile, perfect bubble that held us captive.

But we didn't. We stayed in the stillness, suspended in that fragile, perfect moment. And I knew, without being told, that he would wait until I moved first, a silent agreement that hung in the air like a promise.

When I pulled back, it wasn't a retreat. It was something gentler, a subtle shift that acknowledged the depth of what had just passed between us, a dance of shadows and light that spoke of a connection that transcended the boundaries of the night.

"Stay," I whispered, the word a soft invitation that held a world of meaning.

He didn't ask for a blanket or a reason. He just nodded and curled beside me on the rug, shoulder to shoulder, our mugs untouched and cooling beside us, a silent testament to the night's magic. Whisker took the space between us like a sentry, a silent guardian of our shared peace, his presence a comforting anchor in the sea of emotions that swirled around us.

101

And I closed my eyes to the sound of his breathing, the gentle rhythm lulling me into a state of quiet contentment, a soft melody that whispered of the night's secrets, a lullaby that sang me to sleep, wrapped in the warmth of a connection that transcended the boundaries of time and space.

Chapter 14: The Dreaming Shelf

I woke before the light changed, as the night began to dissolve into a soft, gray dawn. The room was quiet, save for the gentle rhythm of breath—mine and his, syncopating softly in the stillness.

Aurelian was still beside me, his body warm and his presence even warmer. One arm was curled protectively around Whisker, who looked thoroughly pleased with himself, tucked between us like the center of some unspoken vow. The cat's purrs were low and steady, a comforting metronome ticking away the seconds until daybreak.

The fire hadn't been lit, and yet the room was warm. Not from magic. Not from spellwork. From breath and nearness. From the heat of bodies close and comfortable, from tea left half-sipped on the table, and from a shared silence that hadn't yet unraveled with the morning light.

I didn't move right away. I let my gaze linger on Aurelian, tracing the lines of his face, the curve of his jaw, the way his lashes caught the soft gray of pre-dawn like dewdrops on a spider's web. His hair had fallen across his brow, a dark curtain drawn over thought, hiding his dreams from the waking world. He looked peaceful in a way that made something tender catch behind my ribs, a soft ache that felt both sweet and sorrowful.

He'd stayed.

That truth hummed louder than any spell, resonating within me like the echo of a sacred song. It was a simple fact, but it held a power that made my heart swell.

When he finally stirred, it was slow, like the first tendrils of dawn stretching across the sky. There were no words at first, just the rustle of a stretch and a soft, sleep-thick hum that seemed to vibrate through his chest. His hand found mine easily, not deliberately, but as if it had always meant to be there, a natural extension of his own body.

"I had a dream," he murmured, his voice still grainy with sleep, like gravel under soft rain.

"Tell me," I urged, my voice barely above a whisper, as if speaking too loudly might shatter the delicate moment.

He smiled, eyes still closed, as if savoring the remnants of his dream. "We were sitting right here. Same tea. Same cat. But the books were singing." His voice held a hint of wonder, like a child describing a magical world only they could see.

104

I blinked, my brows furrowing slightly. "That... doesn't sound entirely like a dream," I said, my mind already racing with possibilities.

He opened one eye, a glint of curiosity sparking in his gaze. "Oh?"

I reached over and picked up the candle from the edge of the rug—the one I'd burned for memoryleaf. The wax had cooled in waves, rippled like water caught mid-whisper, frozen in time and space.

"That's a dream-calling candle," I explained, holding it up for him to see. "It catches echoes. Pieces of dreams, fragments of memories. It's not just a dream if it's trying to tell you something."

He sat up slowly, his brows raised in surprise. "You never cease to surprise me," he said, his voice filled with a mix of admiration and disbelief.

"I'm a bookseller. Not a mystery," I replied, a small smile playing at the corners of my mouth.

He shook his head, his gaze never leaving mine. "You're both," he insisted, his voice firm with conviction.

We shared the rest of the morning in our usual way—slow tea, soft bread, a quiet that didn't need apology or explanation. I let him help feed Whisker, which was a far greater act of trust than I let on. The cat wound around his ankles, purring loudly, as if giving his own seal of approval. Aurelian moved with a familiarity that made my heart ache, as if he had always been here, always been a part of this little world I'd carved out for myself.

He made himself a second cup of tea without asking where things were. He already knew. He knew where the tea was kept, where the cups were stacked, and how I liked my tea.

The moment that nearly made me cry wasn't some dramatic gesture or grand declaration. It was when he reached for the chipped mug I always used and poured it first. Gave it to me without a word, just a soft smile that held a world of understanding. It was the kind of knowing that could only come from paying attention, from seeing the little things that made up the fabric of my life and honoring them.

And then, while sorting through some books left behind after the festival, I found it.

The book was small and unmarked, tucked away in a corner as if waiting to be discovered. It was bound in pale leather, the color of sun-bleached bones, with a single gold thread along the spine that caught the light like a secret whispered in the dark. There was no title, no author's name etched into the cover. But when I opened it, my name was there, written in a hand that made my breath catch in my throat.

Not *Elowen Thistlewhim*, the name I'd chosen for myself, the name that held my power and my identity. But *Elowenna*. A name I hadn't heard since I was a child. A name only my father used.

The inscription was in his handwriting, the letters looping and flowing like a dance only he knew the steps to.

To Elowenna, for the days you feel like a story too quiet to be told.

I ran my fingers over the ink, tracing the curves and lines as if they were a map to a forgotten land. It didn't smudge. Which meant it had been sealed. Protected. A message from the past, preserved for this very moment.

The pages that followed weren't printed. They were handwritten, each word carefully crafted, each letter a testament to the time and care he'd taken. It was a collection of dream fragments, folk stories, poems woven with runes I only half-recognized. It was a book of dreams. My father's dreams.

"I didn't know this was here," I whispered, my voice barely audible, as if speaking too loudly might shatter the delicate moment.

Aurelian moved closer, his presence a comforting warmth at my back. "Was it yours?" he asked, his voice soft with curiosity.

I shook my head, my gaze still fixed on the pages before me. "I think it was waiting," I said, my voice filled with a sense of awe and wonder. "Waiting for me to find it."

We spent the rest of the day cataloging it gently, page by page, as if handling something fragile and precious. Some of the stories were clearly metaphors, their meanings hidden behind layers of symbolism and imagery. Others read like maps, guiding the way to places only the dreamer could go. One page was just a sketch of a cat that looked an awful lot like Whisker, dated three years before I was born. It was as if my father had seen into the future, had known that one day, this cat would be a part of my life.

"I think this might be a dreaming shelf book," I murmured, my voice filled with a sense of reverence.

He looked at me, his eyes reflecting the same sense of awe that filled my own. "You mean one that appears when you're ready?" he asked, his voice barely above a whisper.

I nodded, my gaze drifting back to the pages before me. "Or when it's ready for you," I said, my voice filled with a sense of destiny, as if this moment had been written in the stars long before I was born.

Whisker yawned loudly from his perch on the windowsill, as if to say, *Obviously*. His tail flicked lazily, a punctuation mark to his nonchalant agreement.

That night, after he left—after another warm, lingering touch of his hand in mine, a promise of connection and understanding—I sat at the counter and lit the memoryleaf candle again. The flame flickered to life, casting dancing shadows on the walls, as if the very room was alive with the echoes of dreams and memories.

But I didn't write anything down. Instead, I opened my father's dream book and whispered one line aloud from a half-finished page, my voice barely above a whisper, as if speaking to the very heart of the book itself.

"Some roots don't need light to grow. Only a little quiet. And

someone to sit beside them long enough to notice."

I think Aurelian would understand that. I think he already does. The way he sees me, the way he pays attention to the little things, the way he knows me—it's as if he's been sitting beside my roots, nurturing them with his quiet presence, his gentle understanding. It's as if he's been helping me grow, one whispered dream at a time.

Chapter 15: The Book Between Seasons

It began with a thread. A simple, unassuming thing, yet it sparked a cascade of memories and emotions, like a single spark that ignites a wildfire. I found it tucked between the pages of my father's dream book—one I hadn't seen before. It wasn't part of the original binding; it had been added later, like a secret note left in silence, waiting to be discovered. A placeholder, marking a moment in time, a thought interrupted, or perhaps a promise yet to be fulfilled. The thread was gold, stitched with a precision that spoke of care and intention, its mere presence a whisper of the past, a beacon calling me to explore its significance.

And suddenly, with a clarity that startled me, I knew what I wanted to do. It was as if the thread had unraveled a path before me, illuminating a direction I hadn't known I was seeking. The realization was abrupt, yet it felt as natural as breathing, a decision that had been waiting to be made.

I spent the next three days weaving something quiet and meaningful. Each evening, after the shop closed and the last customer departed, leaving behind the bustle of the day, I gathered materials, selecting each one with care. There were pressed leaves, their veins still visible like tiny rivers frozen in time, each one a testament to the seasons that had passed. Scraps of hand-dyed paper, their edges soft and colors muted, reminiscent of the gentle hues of a sunset. Slivers of our favorite shared pages, words and images blending into a patchwork of memories, each fragment a piece of our shared history. Bits of ribbon from the Lantern Market, their hues vibrant against the duller tones of the shop, like bursts of laughter in a quiet room. Even a petal from the flower he'd left on the bridge railing, its fragility a stark contrast to the sturdier elements, a delicate reminder of a moment shared.

I bound each element into a small, hand-stitched journal, the cover soft and inviting, like a well-worn path leading to a familiar place. Not for notes. Not for spells. For *us*. A book of beginnings, a testament to the moments shared and those yet to come, a chronicle of our journey together.

Each page held something small but significant: a line of overheard tea-scented dialogue, the words lingering like a sweet aroma, a fragment of a conversation that had once filled the air. A pressed memory, the details etched into the fibers of the paper, as if the very essence of the moment had been captured and preserved. A sketch of Whisker, his expression unimpressed, as usual, capturing his essence perfectly, a reminder of the constant presence that had witnessed our story unfold. Or a charm for safe travels, the ink shimmering with unspoken hopes, a silent prayer for the journeys that lay ahead. One page was left blank on purpose, with a note written in my own hand: "For whatever we remember next—together." A promise of more adventures, more memories to be made and recorded.

By the third night, as I tied off the last stitch, I realized what I was doing wasn't just crafting a gift. It was a plea, a silent entreaty, a hope whispered into the pages. I was asking him to stay, to be a part of the story that was still being written, to join me on the path that lay before us.

I wrapped it in linen, the fabric smooth and cool under my fingers, like the touch of a tranquil stream. I tied it with that same gold thread, the one that had started it all, a symbol of the journey that had led me here. Simple. No spell. No seal. Just something made slowly, honestly, with every stitch a whisper of my heart's desire, a testament to the love and care that had gone into its creation.

113

Whisker sat on the front counter, his tail flicking in that way that always made me feel like he was judging my hesitation. His green eyes seemed to hold a world of wisdom and a hint of impatience, as if he knew what was to come and was waiting for me to catch up.

"I know," I whispered, more to myself than to him. "Just give me a minute."

The sky outside was streaked with that perfect late-autumn lavender, the kind that smells like woodsmoke and quiet farewells. The kind of evening you notice even if you're trying not to, its beauty insistent, demanding attention, a backdrop that seemed to reflect the emotions swirling within me.

So of course, that's when the bell rang, its chime echoing through the shop, announcing his arrival. The sound was both a comfort and a portent, a signal that the moment of truth had come.

He looked tired when he walked in—not in the way of someone weary from a long day, but someone softened by the world, molded by experiences beyond these walls. His hair was wind-tousled, strands of it catching the light, like golden threads woven into a tapestry of his journey. His hands were stained with something green

114

and herbal, the scent earthy and fresh, a reminder of the grove that called to him, the place that held a part of his heart.

"Ritual harvest," he said before I could ask, his voice carrying the weight of the grove, the echo of the ancient trees and the wisdom they held. "The grove sent for me."

"Everything alright?" I asked, concern edging my voice, a whisper of the fears that had begun to take root in my heart.

He hesitated, then nodded, a small smile playing at the corners of his mouth, a reassurance that held a hint of uncertainty. "They want me to stay for the winter."

Something clenched in my chest, a tightness that made it hard to breathe, as if the very air had become a burden. I swallowed, trying to find the right words, the ones that would convey the depth of my feelings, the hope and the fear that warred within me.

"Do you want to?" I asked, my voice barely above a whisper, a question that held a thousand unspoken words, a plea for him to choose me, to choose us.

He didn't answer immediately. He looked at me instead, his gaze steady and deep, like he was waiting for the question under the question, the one I hadn't yet voiced, the one that held the true weight of my heart.

"I was going to ask you something," I blurted out, the words tumbling from my lips before I could stop them, a confession that had been building within me, a hope that I could no longer contain. "But now I'm not sure it's fair."

"Ask me anyway," he said, his voice gentle, encouraging, a beacon of hope in the storm of my emotions, a promise that he would listen, that he would understand.

I reached behind the counter, my fingers brushing against the parcel, the culmination of my hopes and dreams, the embodiment of my love for him. I brought it out, setting it gently between us, an offering, a plea, a testament to the journey we had shared and the one I hoped we would continue.

"I made you something. It's... a kind of record. Of here. Of us." A chronicle of our love, a testament to the moments that had brought us together, a promise of the adventures that lay ahead.

He touched the edge of the linen wrap with reverence, his fingers tracing the outline of the book hidden within, a silent acknowledgment of the care and love that had gone into its creation. "You made me a book?"

"I made us a book," I said, my voice steady despite the whirlwind of emotions inside me, a declaration of my love, a promise of the future I hoped we would share. "For if you stay. Or if you go and need to remember why you'd want to come back."

His throat worked in a silent swallow, the muscles taut with unspoken words, a reflection of the emotions that held him in their grip, the hopes and fears that mirrored my own.

"Elowen," he said, my name a soft exhale, a sigh filled with a thousand meanings, a testament to the journey we had shared, the love that had grown between us, the hopes and dreams that had taken root in our hearts.

I braced myself, steeling my heart against the expected rejection, preparing for the pain that I feared would follow, the disappointment that would come with the realization that our paths were meant to diverge.

But he didn't say no.

He didn't say yes, either.

He said something better.

"I was going to ask *you* to come with me. Just for the week. So you'd see the grove. So I could show you the part of me that only makes sense when the roots call." An invitation, a promise, a testament to the love that had grown between us, the bond that had formed despite the distance that had once separated us.

I stared at him, heart thudding in my chest, each beat echoing his words, a symphony of hope and love that resonated within me, a promise of the future that lay before us.

"That way," he said, voice barely above a whisper, a soft plea, a testament to the love that had brought us together, the journey that had led us to this moment, the future that lay before us, waiting to be written. "You wouldn't be a chapter I left behind. You'd be part of the next one."

I stepped around the counter before I could overthink it, took his hand in mine, and whispered, "I'm not a bookmark, Leafheart. I'm a story too." A declaration of my love, a promise of the future I hoped we would share, a testament to the journey that had led us to this moment, the path that lay before us, waiting to be explored.

He smiled, his eyes full of that quiet brightness I was learning to love, a light that promised adventures and shared memories, a future filled with love and laughter, a journey that we would take together.

"Then let's write it slowly," he said, his voice a soft promise, a testament to the love that had grown between us, the bond that had formed despite the challenges that had come our way, the future that lay before us, waiting to be written, one page at a time, one memory at a time, one adventure at a time. "Together." A promise of a future filled with love and laughter, a journey that we would take together, a story that was ours to write, ours to live, ours to share.

Chapter 16: Before the Grove

Some places carry memory. They're not the kind of memories you find printed in the pages of history books or forced into the glass vessels of light bulbs. No, these are the memories that seem to breathe on their own, when no one is looking, when silence is the only witness. They're the kind that wait, that bide their time until you return, and then, softly, they ask: Are you sure you want to disturb the past?

The grove is one of those places. It asked me that question today, its voice a rustle of leaves, a whisper of wind. And I answered, with a quiet resolve, yes.

I spent the morning in a silence that wasn't ceremonial or forced, but natural, comfortable. It was a stillness that allowed the wind to move through me without needing to be shaped or directed. The heart-tree, the ancient sentinel of the grove, was already awake when I arrived. Its roots throbbed with a pulse I hadn't felt since my childhood days. It knew I was bringing someone new, someone special. It didn't ask who. It already knew her name.

I prepared the grove carefully, respectfully. I trimmed back the brambles that had grown wild and free between the memory bulbs, their thorns pricking my fingers like tiny reminders of the past. I raked away the frost-leaves that had gathered around the central stones, their crystalline crunch under my feet a rhythm older than time. I lit a line of moss-lanterns with a combination of breath and matchstick magic, just enough to illuminate the path for her, but not so much that it would overwhelm the familiar darkness of the grove.

The grove doesn't take kindly to being overly adorned or fussed over. It prefers to be trusted, to be respected as it is. Much like Elowen. I found myself thinking about her, not in a way that brought a pang of longing, but in the way you notice the soft, gentle things before you realize you've been yearning for them all along. I wondered about the fall of her sleeves, the way she absentmindedly brushes her hair back when she's deep in thought, the small, almost inaudible sound she makes when a passage in a book catches her off guard.

She carries a kind of magic that isn't loud or flashy. It's the kind that makes you want to slow down, to speak softly, to linger a little longer. So, I made space. Not just in the grove, but within myself. I created a place for her in the quiet corners of my being.

Before I left, I rooted one more memory bulb into the earth. It was the first I'd crafted in many months. Inside it, I placed her name, whispered in my breath. I stored the memory of her shop in the rain, the cozy warmth of it a stark contrast to the cold outside. I captured the moment she handed me a cup without asking what I needed, her intuition a balm to my weary soul.

I placed the bulb near the heart-tree, its glass surface reflecting the soft glow of the moss-lanterns. And I whispered, "Please recognize her." Not because she needs the grove's approval, but because I do. Because I need to know that this place, this keeper of memories, understands the significance of her presence. Because I need to know that it's not just me who sees the magic she carries.

Chapter 17: The Grove That Waited

We left at dawn, while the first light of day was just beginning to caress the rooftops of Faerrow. The town was still draped in a blue-gray mist, lending it an air of quiet mystery. I locked the shop door behind me, the click of the latch echoing through the empty street. Upstairs, in the window, Whisker remained curled in a tight ball, his tail twitching intermittently as he chased dream-mice. He knew I'd come back; his calm demeanor was a testament to the trust we shared.

I had packed light for the journey, taking only a worn leather satchel containing the essentials: my favorite cardigan, the one with the frayed cuffs that held the scent of home, a journal bound in leather with pages filled with thoughts and sketches, two bundles of dried tea leaves wrapped carefully in cloth, and the book I had made for Aurelian—our book, filled with shared stories and secrets. Aurelian carried the rest of our supplies, as I knew he would. He was always prepared, always steady.

The path to the grove wound through a part of the forest I rarely visited. Not because it was forbidden, but because it always felt like the forest itself decided when it was ready to be seen. That morning, beneath the soft light of the rising sun, it was ready. The trees seemed to part gently, inviting us in, their leaves whispering secrets in the breeze.

Aurelian didn't speak much as we walked, and neither did I. It wasn't an uncomfortable silence; rather, it was the kind that settles over shared breath, the kind that wraps around you like fog and leaf-filtered light. His hand brushed against mine once, then again, and this time, it stayed there, his fingers intertwining with mine as naturally as the roots beneath our feet.

The deeper we ventured into the forest, the more it seemed to shift around us. The air changed, growing heavier, but not in a burdensome way. It felt rich, ancient, as if the very soil knew our names and welcomed us back. The colors seemed more vibrant, the scents more pronounced—the earthy aroma of damp soil, the sweet perfume of distant flowers, the sharp tang of pine needles.

"We're close," Aurelian murmured, his voice barely above a whisper, as if he didn't want to disturb the tranquility of the woods.

He led me down a slope so gentle that I barely noticed the descent until the trees opened up around us, revealing a sight that stole my breath away.

The grove.

It was unlike anything I had imagined. Not grand, not otherworldly, but deeply, profoundly alive. The clearing was ringed by sentinel trees—ancient, knotted things with bark like braided rope and leaves that shimmered with a faint, ethereal magic. A stream cut through the middle, its water so clear that I could see the golden-veined stones beneath the surface, smoothed by time and water. Moss-covered stones circled a central space, and at the heart of it all stood a low, wide tree with a hollow core and roots that pulsed rhythmically, like the steady beat of a heart.

"I grew up here," Aurelian said, standing beside me, his voice filled with reverence and memories. "Every season, every change—I came here before I could read and stayed long after I knew how to leave."

I stepped closer to the heart-tree, my fingers hovering over its bark, feeling the hum of life beneath my touch. "It feels... like something is remembering," I said softly, trying to put into words the sensation that coursed through me.

"It is," he replied, his gaze on the tree. "This grove listens. And it never forgets who touches it with intention."

I pressed my hand to the bark, feeling its warmth, its history. It was as if the tree itself breathed, its life force mingling with mine.

We spent the day exploring the grove, Aurelian showing me its secrets and wonders. He led me to the archive roots—where he stored memories in earth-bound vessels. Tiny glass bulbs planted like seeds, each one tied to a moment, a feeling, a truth. He dug one up gently, holding it out to me with care.

"This one's mine," he said, a soft smile playing on his lips. "From the first day I stepped into your shop."

I stared at the pale glow within the bulb, a tangible piece of our past held in my hand. "You kept that?" I asked, my voice barely above a whisper.

"I rooted it," he said softly, his eyes meeting mine. "So I wouldn't forget what it felt like to be seen. To be truly seen."

My throat tightened, emotion welling up inside me. I reached into my satchel, pulled out our book, and placed it at the base of the

126

heart-tree. "For safekeeping," I said, my voice steady despite the whirlwind of feelings within me.

Aurelian didn't speak. He just reached out and brushed his fingers across mine, a gentle touch that spoke volumes. Together, we watched as the roots of the heart-tree slowly curled around the book's cover, embracing it like a promise being held.

As evening crept into the grove, painting the sky with muted lavender hues, Aurelian lit a soft flame from dried moss and leaf-ribbons. We sat beside it, our backs pressed against the tree, the warmth between us not just from the fire but from something deeper, something more profound.

"I've never brought anyone here," he said, his voice just above the whisper of the wind through the leaves. "Not even when I thought I might be in love once."

I turned to him slowly, my gaze meeting his. "Why me?" I asked, the question hanging in the air between us.

"Because when I'm with you," he said, his eyes never leaving mine, "I remember who I am when I'm not trying to be anything. When I'm not trying to fit into someone else's expectations or mold. I'm just... me."

127

My heart broke open in the softest way, like the first light of dawn breaking through the darkness. No fanfare, no rush—just a gentle, inevitable unfolding.

I reached up and cupped his cheek, the way I'd wanted to for days, feeling the rough stubble against my palm. And this time, he didn't wait. He leaned in, his lips meeting mine in a kiss that was soft and real and warm, like the first light on old bark.

When we broke apart, we stayed close, forehead to forehead, hands entwined. The world around us seemed to fade away, leaving only the two of us in this sacred space.

"I don't know what this will look like in spring," I whispered, my voice barely audible.

"We'll find out," he said, his thumb tracing patterns on the back of my hand. "One page at a time."

And beneath us, the heart-tree pulsed once, content, as if the very forest itself approved of our union, our promise to each other.

Chapter 18: The Root Beneath the Page

When we returned to Faerrow, the town greeted us with an unchanged facade, as if it had been patiently awaiting our arrival, content to remain static in our absence. The cobblestones glistened beneath our feet, still damp from the previous night's mist, reflecting the muted glow of the afternoon sun like a thousand tiny, shimmering mirrors. The smoke from the chimneys spiraled lazily into the air, performing an unhurried dance, twisting and turning in the gentle breeze before dissipating into the crisp autumn air. Perched on the bookstore awning, the same old crow watched us with beady, disinterested eyes, his feathers ruffling slightly in the breeze, as if he had nowhere else to be and nothing better to do than observe the comings and goings of the townsfolk below.

Yet, despite the familiarity of the scene before me, something within me had shifted. It wasn't a dramatic change, not like the sudden clap of thunder that splits the sky or the stark metamorphosis of a caterpillar into a butterfly. Instead, it was quiet, almost imperceptible—a deeper breath, an expansion of the lungs, a subtle unfurling of something that had long been held tight. Like a root that had decided to stretch a little farther into the soil, anchoring itself more firmly in the earth, drawing in nourishment and life from the depths below.

Whisker greeted us at the door, arching his back in an exaggerated stretch, his fur standing on end as if electrified. He sauntered over to Aurelian's boots, sniffing them with the meticulousness of a seasoned investigator, his tiny nose twitching as he paused at the unfamiliar scents of moss and grove-flame that clung to the leather. Satisfied with his findings, he promptly retreated to his favorite spot in the window nook, curling into a tight ball with a low *huff* of approval, his purrs filling the silence of the room like a soft, gentle melody.

Aurelian and I exchanged few words as we began to unpack our belongings, the silence between us comfortable and familiar. He carefully placed the last of his glass memory bulbs in the corner window, allowing the fading sunlight to catch their faint, ethereal glow, casting prisms of light onto the worn wooden floor. I, on the other hand, moved instinctively to set the kettle to boil, more out of habit than any particular need for tea. The ritual was comforting, the simple act of filling the kettle and setting it on the stove a soothing balm to my restless spirit.

As I passed the mirror near the shop counter—the one I usually avoided with deliberate intent, my eyes averted from the reflection that stared back at me—I found myself pausing. My reflection stared back at me, unchanged. The same features, the same expression. Yet, there was something subtly different, something that had softened. Not vanished, but eased, like the gentle release of a long-held tension, the slow unwinding of a tightly coiled rope.

Over steaming cups of tea, the aroma of chamomile and honey filling the air, I voiced the question that had been lingering in my mind. "Do you think the grove gave me something, Aurelian?"

Aurelian raised an eyebrow, his gaze steady over the rim of his cup, his eyes reflecting the flickering light of the candle that sat between us. "What makes you ask, dear one?"

I hesitated, searching for the right word to encapsulate the sensation that had been lingering at the edge of my consciousness. "I've been feeling… attuned," I said finally, the word feeling strange and unfamiliar on my tongue.

"To what?" he prompted, his curiosity piqued, his voice gentle and coaxing.

"Everything," I admitted, setting down my cup, the porcelain clinking softly against the saucer. "The books, the lanterns, even the tea blends. It's like I can hear their *moods*. Like the shop is humming louder, resonating with a life of its own. I can feel it, Aurelian. I can feel it all."

Aurelian smiled, a warm and knowing expression that crinkled the corners of his eyes, his gaze softening as he looked at me. "Then maybe it didn't give you anything, my dear. Maybe it woke something up. Something that was already there, dormant, waiting for the right moment to bloom."

I looked around *Thistle & Thread*, taking in the flickering candles, the way the light curved around the cozy reading nook, the gentle, living hush that filled the air. I had always loved this place, but now, it felt different. It felt alive, pulsating with an energy that seemed to embrace me, to whisper secrets into my ear. I could feel it loving me back, its warmth enveloping me like a comforting embrace.

"You think it was always there?" I asked, my voice barely above a whisper, the words catching in my throat.

132

"I think," Aurelian said gently, his voice filled with a quiet conviction, "you were too busy tending to others to notice your own bloom. Too busy nurturing the world around you to see the beauty that was blossoming within you."

I swallowed hard, a lump forming in my throat. It was strange, being seen so clearly without having to explain anything, without having to justify or rationalize my feelings. Stranger still was the realization of how much I wanted to keep being seen by him, how much I craved his understanding, his acceptance. How much I longed to be known, truly and deeply, by this man who had become such an integral part of my life.

Later, as Aurelian ventured across the square to run an errand, his footsteps echoing softly on the cobblestones, I found myself lingering in the back room. Before me lay a bundle of blank paper and a freshly stitched spine, the raw materials of a new creation. I wasn't making a spellbook this time. No, this was something different, something more personal. Something that was uniquely mine.

I was making *my* book. A journal not of memories already made, but of what was *becoming*. I dipped my pen into the inkwell, the cool liquid clinging to the nib as I poised it above the first page, the anticipation of creation buzzing in my veins. With a slow, deliberate hand, I wrote only one sentence, the words flowing from my heart onto the paper like a river breaking free from its dam.

"The page turned quietly, but everything changed."

That night, Aurelian returned with a single item clutched in his hand. He handed it to me without ceremony, his fingers brushing against mine as he relinquished his hold, the touch sending a jolt of warmth through me. It was a root-carved bookmark, shaped like an open door, its surface smooth and inviting to the touch, the grain of the wood telling a story of time and growth.

"I thought it belonged to your story now," he said, his voice soft yet filled with an unyielding certainty, his eyes reflecting the flickering light of the candles that danced around us.

And I believed him. For in that moment, I understood that my story was not yet written, that the chapters of my life were still unfolding, still waiting to be filled with the adventures and discoveries that lay ahead. With the open door held tightly in my grasp, I felt ready to step forward, to embrace the unknown, to write the tale that was uniquely mine. To claim the story that had been waiting for me all along, the story that was finally ready to be told.

Chapter 19: What the Grove Remembers

She didn't kiss me first. She didn't feel the need to be the initiator, to prove anything or stake a claim. She simply let me. And somehow, that simple act of allowing, of trusting me to make the first move, meant more than any rushed or forced affection could have. It was a quiet, powerful statement—a silent, mutual understanding that transcended words.

The heart-tree has stood for centuries, older than Faerrow, older than any name we could give it. It has witnessed generations, remembered tales untold, and carried secrets whispered by the wind. It remembers soft things—the gentle touch of lovers, the whispered confessions, the silent tears. It remembers wounds, both physical and emotional, and the wishes of countless souls who sought solace in its ancient bark. The press of hands that said "please" and "I'm here" and "don't leave yet" are etched into its very being, a testament to the human condition.

Now, it remembers Elowen too.

She approached the heart-tree with a purpose, her steps deliberate, her touch intentional. She didn't leave behind a spell or a charm—just her presence. And presence, I've come to understand, is the most enduring kind of magic. It's the kind that doesn't need grand gestures or flashy displays. It's the kind that lingers, that changes the very air around it.

She made the grove softer just by walking into it. Her presence brought a warmth that wasn't there before, a comfort that made the ancient trees seem more welcoming. She made me softer, too. Her presence eased the edges of my heart, made me feel a sense of peace I hadn't known in a long time.

After she fell asleep, her head tucked under my chin, Whisker a warm, judgmental loaf near our feet, I didn't move for a long time. Not because I was afraid of waking her, but because I didn't want to forget what it felt like to be chosen back. I wanted to savor this moment, this feeling of being accepted, of being wanted just as I am.

I've known attraction—the fleeting, intense pull that burns hot and fast. I've known infatuation—the heady, intoxicating rush that leaves you breathless. But love? This is different. It doesn't tug at you, doesn't leave you feeling off-balance. It anchors you, grounds you, gives you a sense of belonging that goes beyond mere physical attraction.

When the fire dipped low and the snow began to creep in around the stones, I carefully pulled out our book from my satchel. The leather was worn, the pages filled with our shared memories, our thoughts, our dreams. And I wrote something I hadn't said aloud, something that felt too raw, too real to be spoken.

She doesn't ask me to stay. She doesn't beg or plead, doesn't try to convince me with words or promises. But every time she looks at me, I forget why I ever left anything behind. I forget the reasons I had for wandering, for seeking something more. Because in her eyes, I find a home, a sense of belonging that makes all my wanderlust fade away.

I pressed a clover petal between the pages—a small, delicate token of this moment. It was one I'd tucked into my pocket earlier, when she laughed at the frostroot stains on my hands. Her laughter had been warm, genuine, and it had filled me with a joy I couldn't quite explain.

And I sealed the book—not as a record of our time together, not as a memento to look back on. But as a promise to myself. A promise to remember this feeling, to hold onto it, to cherish it.

The grove will remember her forever now. Her presence has left an indelible mark, a softness that will linger long after she's gone. And so will I. Not as the girl who let me into her heart, but as the one who never tried to keep me. Because she didn't have to. Because she knew, just as I did, that some things are meant to be—that some connections transcend time and space, that they are as eternal and unyielding as the heart-tree itself.

Chapter 20: The First Frost Wish

The first frost had arrived in the quiet of the night, a silent whisper of winter that took the village by surprise. It had descended unseen and unheard, like a secret shared between the moon and the earth, leaving behind a shimmering trail of crystalline beauty. The stillness of the morning was broken only by the faint crunch of frozen leaves underfoot, each step echoing like a hushed whisper in the tranquil air. The world seemed to sparkle with a newfound magic, as if the very breath of winter had cast a spell of serenity over the landscape. As the shopkeeper of the local apothecary, she took a moment to appreciate the delicate beauty of the frost that adorned the windowpanes like intricate silver filigree, a fleeting masterpiece crafted by the chill of the night.

Stepping barefoot onto the shop's wooden floor, she savored the cool sensation beneath her toes, a stark contrast to the warmth that radiated from the hearth. The grain of the wood was smooth and familiar, worn by years of use and the gentle touch of countless feet. The air was filled with the comforting scent of dried herbs and the faint, lingering aroma of the previous day's brews. The First Frost was a significant event in Faerrow, a village where the boundaries between seasons were blurred, and the transitions were met with reverence and celebration. It was a day that held a special place in the hearts of the villagers, a moment when the cycle of the year paused and shifted, ushering in a new phase of life.

The tradition of The First Frost was simple, yet held deep meaning for the villagers. Each person would write their most heartfelt wish on a slip of paper, carefully fold it three times, and tuck it away in a spot where they believed warmth would find it as winter gave way to spring. It was a ritual of hope and anticipation, a collective prayer for the fulfillment of dreams and desires, whispered into the cold air and held close to the heart. The wishes were as varied as the villagers themselves, ranging from hopes for a bountiful harvest to yearnings for love and happiness. Yet, each one was imbued with the same sense of longing and expectation, a silent plea to the universe for a brighter future.

This year, she found herself approaching the tradition with a renewed sense of purpose. In the past, her wishes had been made out of habit, the words flowing easily but without real conviction. They had been fleeting thoughts, barely given form before being folded away and forgotten. This time, however, she had something tangible to hope for, a dream that had taken root in her heart and refused to let go. It was a longing that had grown stronger with each passing day, nurtured by the quiet moments of reflection and the stolen glances that spoke volumes more than words ever could.

As the sun dipped below the horizon and the village square began to twinkle with lantern light, she knew it was time. The soft glow of the lanterns cast dancing shadows on the cobblestone streets, and the air was filled with the hum of quiet conversations and shared laughter. Aurelian, the village's skilled herbalist, had spent the day gathering frost-leaves with the grove-keepers, his satchel now full of delicate herbs and precious root samples. His hands, stained with the earth and the scent of the forest, were a testament to his dedication and love for the craft. He had left her a note that morning, the words pressed into the fragrant thyme leaf that lay on her workbench, a silent promise of shared dreams and unspoken desires.

"Save me a wish."

She hadn't replied, wanting to wait until the moment felt right to commit her heart's desire to paper. And now, as the scents of freshly baked bread and crackling fires filled the air, she knew that moment had come. The village was alive with the spirit of The First Frost, and the atmosphere was electric with the collective hopes and dreams of its inhabitants. It was a night when anything seemed possible, and the future felt ripe with potential.

Back in the cozy confines of the shop, she carefully tore a narrow slip of parchment from the edge of her journal. The paper was creamy and soft, its edges slightly rough and uneven. It was just wide enough to hold the weight of her wish, the ink barely fitting within the confines of the page. Sitting cross-legged beside the fire, she whispered the words as she wrote, infusing them with all the hope and longing that she held within her. The firelight cast a warm glow on her face, illuminating the lines and curves of her handwriting as she poured her heart onto the page.

"Let him stay because he wants to, not because I ask."

The truth of the wish struck her like a physical blow, the realization of how deeply she cared for Aurelian and how much she wanted their lives to be intertwined. It was a longing that went beyond mere affection; it was a deep, soulful connection that seemed to transcend the boundaries of time and space. Folding the paper once,

143

then again, and finally a third time, she tucked it beneath the loose floorboard beside the hearth, the one that seemed to hold the warmth of the fire no matter the season. It was a secret place, a sanctuary for her hopes and dreams, where they could be nurtured and protected until the time was right for them to blossom.

Hours later, as the village had settled into the quiet hush of night, Aurelian returned to the shop. His cheeks were flushed with cold, and his eyes seemed to dance with the light of the fire. The chill of the night clung to his clothes, but his smile was warm and inviting, a beacon of comfort in the darkness. He didn't speak as he crossed the threshold, but the look he gave her spoke volumes. It was as if the day had stretched on for an eternity, and he had finally found his way back to where he belonged. His presence filled the room, bringing with it a sense of completeness and belonging that she had never felt before.

She offered him a steaming mug of Hearthbrew, the warmth radiating from the cup a comforting balm against the chill of the night. The aroma of the brew was rich and soothing, a blend of sweet herbs and fragrant spices that seemed to embody the very essence of home. "Your wish is safe," she said softly, her voice barely more than a

144

whisper. The words hung in the air, a silent promise of shared hopes and dreams.

He accepted the mug with both hands, cradling it close as if it were a precious treasure. The steam rose in delicate tendrils, casting a soft glow on his face and highlighting the lines of fatigue and contentment that etched his features. "And yours?" he asked, his eyes never leaving hers. His voice was low and gentle, a soothing melody that seemed to resonate deep within her soul.

"Hidden," she replied, "but still burning."

He nodded, understanding the depth of her words and the significance of the ritual they had both taken part in. It was a shared secret, a bond that transcended the boundaries of time and space, connecting them on a level that was both profound and intimate. Then, with a quiet smile, he reached into the pocket of his coat and pulled out a small, round object. It pulsed faintly with warmth, the glow barely discernible in the firelight.

A memory bulb.

But this one was different; it wasn't sealed. The surface of the bulb was smooth and translucent, revealing the soft, ethereal light that emanated from within. It was a delicate, fragile thing, a whisper of a dream captured in glass and held suspended in time.

"What is it?" she asked, her curiosity piqued by the unusual artifact. Her voice was barely more than a whisper, a hushed reverence for the secret that lay before her.

He leaned in, his forehead brushing against hers as he whispered, "It's a wish. But I wanted you to see it before it comes true."

And in that moment, as the fire crackled and the village slept, they shared a secret that bound them together, a dream that would carry them through the long winter nights and into the promise of a new beginning. It was a promise of hope and love, of shared dreams and unspoken desires, whispered into the night and held close to the heart. A promise that, like the first frost, would leave its mark on their souls, a delicate, shimmering trail of love and longing that would guide them into the future.

Chapter 21: The Wish I Didn't Write

I held the parchment in my hands for a long time, feeling its rough edges and the subtle creases that marked its age. The color of weak tea, it bore the whispers of countless wishes that had been scribed upon its surface, absorbed into its fibers. I ran my fingers along its edges, letting the silence of the room envelop me.

Folded it once, a crisp crease down the center, bisecting the empty space where words should have been. The sound of the fold was loud in the quiet, a sharp crack that echoed the finality of my decision.

Then again, another fold, this time creating a perfect rectangle, a secret pocket where my thoughts could hide. But the parchment remained blank, untouched by ink or charcoal.

Not because I didn't want something. Oh, there were things I yearned for, things that kept me awake at night, staring into the dark. But because what I wanted was already here, within reach, tangible as the parchment between my fingers.

147

The First Frost had always been a ritual for me, a moment of quiet reflection amidst the chaos of life. Even when I was away from Faerrow, I found some version of it. In the northern colonies, where the cold bites deeper, it was frostmarks etched into the bark of ancestral trees, their silvery lines a stark contrast to the dark wood. In the west woods, where the wind whispered secrets, it was spoken wishes carried on windleaf lanterns, their flickering lights dancing like tiny stars against the night sky.

But it was always the same idea, the same quiet act of hope and longing. Ask for something. Tuck it somewhere warm, somewhere safe, somewhere it could burrow and wait. Wait for the thaw, for the moment when the world awakens and anything seems possible.

This year, I didn't want to ask. I didn't want to add my voice to the chorus of pleas and bargains. I wanted to thank. To express a gratitude that swelled within me like a ripe fruit, sweet and full.

I watched her across the square, her cheeks pink from the cold, her breath misting in the crisp air. Her eyes held that quiet ache I'm starting to recognize as hope, a soft yearning that made my heart

148

clench. She was a vision of warmth amidst the chill, a beacon of light in the fading day.

She didn't see me. She was too absorbed in her own world, too focused on the small piece of paper in her hands. I watched as she folded it carefully, her fingers delicate and precise. She slipped it into her coat pocket, a secret stowed away, a wish tucked against her heart.

Her wish, probably. A silent plea, a whispered dream. I didn't want to know what it said. Not yet. Not until she was ready to share it, to speak it aloud. But I hoped it had my name in it. Even if just in the margins, a footnote in her dreams.

When I got back to the grove that night, the heart-tree stood sentinel, its ancient branches reaching out like welcoming arms. I sat beneath it, the rough bark against my back, the cool earth beneath me. I whispered my wish out loud anyway, not to the silent soil or the whispering wind, but to her.

Wherever she was in that moment—upstairs in the shop, the warm glow of the window casting her in silhouette, brushing Whisker off the window ledge with a gentle hand, steeping her tea just right, the scent of herbs filling the air—I whispered my plea.

"Please don't change. Not for me. Not for anyone. Just let me stay long enough to become someone worthy of the way you see me. Let me grow into the man you believe I am."

I pressed the blank parchment between the roots anyway, tucking it into the heart of the tree. Let the grove decide what to do with it. Let the ancient magic of the place guide it. Because maybe not wishing is its own kind of vow, a promise to accept what is and what will be. A pledge to be grateful, to be present, to be enough.

Chapter 22: The Gathering Light

The Winter Gathering was never a grand affair, not in the way that many other festivals were. There were no vibrant banners snapping in the crisp wind, no long-winded speeches from esteemed figures, and certainly no pageantry that screamed of pomp and circumstance. Instead, it was a quiet, almost unassuming event that held a unique charm, a subtle magic that made it dear to the hearts of those who attended.

The communal fire in the center of the town square was the main attraction, casting long, dancing shadows that painted the cobblestones with a warm, inviting glow. Mugs of mulled cider were passed from hand to hand, the sweet, spicy aroma filling the air and mingling with the soft, gentle music that seemed to be everywhere and nowhere all at once. It wasn't music that demanded attention; it simply existed, a harmonious backdrop to the quiet conversations and warm smiles shared among the townsfolk.

I loved it. I loved how Faerrow didn't need permission to be gentle, how it didn't require grandeur or opulence to bring people together. There was a beauty in its simplicity, a comfort in its familiarity. And yet, this year, I found myself hesitating at the threshold of my home, my hand lingering on the doorframe as I looked out at the gathering night.

Maybe it was because everything within me felt fuller, more alive, like a river swollen with rain, its banks straining to contain the rush of water. I felt more fragile, more luminous, as if I were a delicate glass vessel filled to the brim with light. The kind of full that trembles at the slightest touch, that doesn't want to be seen unless it's by someone who understands, someone who won't ask you to shrink or dim your light.

Aurelian seemed to sense my hesitation, offering his hand the moment I stepped outside, his breath misting in the chilly air. "You don't have to go," he said softly, his eyes reflecting the distant glow of the communal fire. "Not if you're not ready."

I looked at his outstretched hand, then up at his face, his features etched with concern and understanding. "I want to," I replied, my voice barely above a whisper. "I just... don't know how to be in it yet."

"In what?" he asked, his head tilting slightly as he studied me.
152

"This," I said, gesturing vaguely between us. "Us."

He didn't let go of my hand, his fingers warm and steadfast around mine. "Then don't be in it like it's something you have to carry," he said, his voice gentle yet firm. "Be in it like a fire you're allowed to sit beside. Feel its warmth, let it comfort you, but don't think you have to tend to it alone."

The town square was already bathed in a soft, inviting light by the time we arrived, the sun having dipped below the horizon, leaving the lanterns to take over its duty. They hung from trees and windows, their shapes mimicking leaves, books, and tea kettles, casting a warm, comforting glow over the proceedings. Children passed around firefruit candies, their excited laughter filling the air as the treats glowed faintly when bitten, casting eerie, playful shadows on their smiling faces.

Mr. Wrenly, the kind-faced baker, passed me a slice of cranberry pie without charging, his eyes crinkling at the corners as he winked and said, "For the girl who made Aurelian stop leaving." I didn't know how to respond to that, how to put into words the mix of emotions that welled up inside me at his words. So, I simply smiled, feeling a warm ache spread through my chest, the best kind of ache, one that spoke of belonging and acceptance.

Aurelian drifted into a circle of grove-tenders, their faces illuminated by the soft glow of the nearby lanterns as they discussed frostroot harvesting and memory-preservation techniques. I watched from a distance, sipping my cider, my fingers curled around the warm clay mug like a shield, a barrier between me and the world.

That's when I saw him. Not Aurelian, but someone else. Someone who made my heart stutter and my breath catch in my throat. A man standing near the edge of the square, partially hidden in the shadows cast by the lanterns overhead. He was taller than I remembered, his once dark hair now streaked with gray at the temples. But there was no mistaking that familiar posture, that slight hesitation before every word, that way of standing as if he wasn't quite sure the earth would hold him.

My father. Or someone who looked far too much like him to be mere coincidence.

He didn't approach me, didn't call out or wave. He just stood there, watching me with an intensity that made my heart ache. Then, he gave the smallest of nods, a nod full of unspoken questions and

154

apologies, full of the kind of grief that only belongs to those who disappeared without warning, without explanation.

My breath hitched, and the mug trembled in my hands, the warm cider threatening to spill over the rim. I didn't walk toward him, didn't run or call out. I just stood there, rooted to the spot, letting the frost bite at my throat as I wondered if he was real, if this was truly happening, or if the memoryleaf candle I'd lit the night before had pulled something through from the past, something I wasn't ready to face.

By the time Aurelian returned to my side, his brow furrowed with concern, the space where the man had stood was empty, nothing but shadows remaining. I looked up at Aurelian, my eyes wide and filled with uncertainty, but I couldn't find the words to explain what I'd seen, what I'd felt.

I didn't speak for a long while, not until we were back at the shop, the familiar scent of herbs and books enveloping me like a comforting embrace. Not until the fire was lit, its warm glow chasing away the shadows that seemed to cling to my skin. Not until Whisker, my faithful feline companion, curled up beside me, his eyes narrowed as if he, too, had seen something he couldn't quite name, something that lingered just beyond the reach of understanding.

"I saw someone tonight," I whispered, the words finally breaking free from the tight confines of my throat. Aurelian didn't push, didn't press for more. He just waited, his expression open and patient, giving me the space I needed to find the words.

"My father," I said, my voice barely audible. "I think."

His expression shifted, softening with concern but remaining alert, ready to listen, ready to support. "Think or know?" he asked gently.

I swallowed hard, my fingers curling into the fabric of my skirt. "I don't know what's real anymore when it comes to him," I admitted, my voice trembling slightly. "But something in me... recognized him. Not with sight. With ache."

Aurelian nodded slowly, then reached into his satchel and pulled out the memory bulb I'd never opened, the one he'd given me after the First Frost. It glowed softly in his hand, its light pulsating gently, almost soothingly. "This is still yours," he said, his voice soft yet steady. "And you don't have to open it until you're ready."

I took the memory bulb from him, feeling its warmth spread through my fingers, up my arm, and into my chest. I curled around it, holding it close like a precious treasure, a lifeline to a past I wasn't sure I was ready to face. "What if I'm never ready?" I whispered, my voice filled with fear and uncertainty.

"Then I'll sit with you anyway," Aurelian replied, his voice filled with conviction and unwavering support. And I believed him. I believed that no matter what happened, no matter what I chose to do, he would be there, steady and constant as the sunrise, ready to face the dawn with me.

Chapter 23: The Pages We Keep

I didn't sleep. Not even a fleeting moment of drowsiness visited me. I lay awake, staring into the darkness, my mind a whirlwind of thoughts that refused to quiet down. It wasn't fear that kept me alert—just a mind too full, thoughts pressing against one another like pages in an overstuffed book, each clamoring for my attention. The night had been an endless carousel of memories and speculations, each hour blurring into the next until time lost all meaning.

When the first light of morning finally began to filter through the window, I lit only one candle. Its scent, a blend of memoryleaf and clove, filled the room with a comforting aroma that seemed to whisper tales of the past. I let the candle burn low, watching the flame dance and flicker as if it, too, were trying to tell a story. I sat beside the hearth, the warmth of the fire a stark contrast to the cool smoothness of the unopened memory bulb in my hands.

The bulb pulsed faintly, rhythmically, like a heartbeat sealed within its transparent walls. It was a silent, steady reminder of the secrets it held, the echoes of a voice I hadn't heard in years. Each pulse seemed to resonate with my own heart, a silent conversation between the past and the present.

Aurelian moved about the room with a quiet grace, his presence a comforting backdrop to my introspection. He didn't rush me or try to fill the silence with empty words. Instead, he went about his morning routine, the soft clink of the kettle and the rustle of tea leaves a soothing melody that complemented the dance of the candle flame. He fed Whisker, who purred contentedly at his feet, his agile body leaning into Aurelian's touch. As Aurelian passed behind me, he paused just long enough to kiss the top of my head, a gentle, fleeting touch that spoke volumes of his understanding and patience. He didn't ask any questions, didn't press for answers. He simply let me be, giving me the space I needed to wrestle with my thoughts.

But the bulb seemed to grow warmer, more insistent, each time I hesitated. It was as if it sensed my apprehension, my fear of the emotions it might unleash. The rhythm of its pulse seemed to quicken, urging me to make a decision. And finally, with a whisper that was barely audible even to myself, I said, "Alright."

The memory bulb opened in a burst of light. Soft, pulsing gold poured from the glass, unfurling into the air like mist on a cold morning. The light seemed to breathe, expanding and contracting with a rhythm that matched the beating of my own heart. It filled the room, casting a warm glow over the familiar surroundings, transforming them into a tableau of memory and emotion.

Then, a voice.

Not present, not physical, but recorded in the way only rootbound memory could hold—an echo shaped by emotion, magic, and the passage of time. It was a voice that carried the weight of years, the echo of a love that transcended time and distance. It resonated through the room, through me, stirring memories I had long thought buried.

"Elowenna," the voice said, and the sound of my name was like a key turning in a long-forgotten lock, opening a door to a part of myself I had thought lost. It was a voice I hadn't heard in years, yet it was as familiar as my own. It was the voice of my father.

And I broke.

Tears blurred the room, turning the familiar surroundings into a watercolor of memory and emotion. I didn't try to stop them. I let

160

them fall, each one a testament to the years of longing, the years of wondering. They were a release, a acknowledgment of the pain I had carried for so long.

The voice continued, soft and sure, a beacon in the storm of my emotions. Each word was carefully chosen, a message crafted with love and intention.

"If this ever reaches you, I want you to know—I didn't mean to go. I followed a story into the deep woods, and the story swallowed me. Not with cruelty, but with purpose. The grove held me, changed me. And in the end, asked me to let go. Of everything except the love I carried for you."

His words painted a picture in my mind, a story within a story. I could see him, my father, drawn into the heart of the woods, compelled by a force he couldn't resist. I could see the grove, ancient and wise, its roots deep and its branches reaching for the sky. And I could see him, changed, transformed, yet still holding onto the love that bound us together.

The light began to fade, the pulsing gold retreating back into the glass as if satisfied that its message had been delivered. The room stilled, the air heavy with the weight of the past and the promise of the future. The candle flickered one last time before going out, leaving only the soft glow of the dying embers in the hearth.

And I wept.

Not for the past, not for the years lost or the words left unsaid. But for the part of me that had never stopped wondering whether I was worth staying for, whether I was enough. For the part of me that had never stopped hoping, never stopped loving, never stopped waiting.

When I finally looked up, Aurelian was sitting across from me, his eyes reflecting the dying embers of the fire. He was silent, open, a presence that didn't flinch from pain but embraced it, understood it. He had been there all along, a steady constant in the storm of my emotions.

"I don't need answers," I whispered, my voice raw from tears and emotion. "I just needed a goodbye."

He reached out, his hand warm and steady as it enveloped mine. His touch was an anchor, a lifeline pulling me back from the depths of my sorrow. "Then maybe now," he said, his voice a gentle anchor in the storm, "you can write the next page."

I returned the dream book to its shelf, my fingers tracing the worn spine with a sense of finality. I didn't hide it away, didn't seal it shut as if to lock away the past. Instead, I placed our book—the one I made for Aurelian, filled with our shared memories and dreams—on top of it. Because sometimes healing isn't about choosing which memory wins, which part of the past gets to define us. It's about choosing which memories we bring with us, which stories we let shape our future.

As I stepped back, looking at the two books side by side, I knew that I was ready to write the next chapter, ready to live the next part of my story. The past would always be a part of me, but it no longer defined me. I was more than my memories, more than my losses. I was my own story, and I was ready to tell it.

Chapter 24: A Room for Winter

Winter crept in slowly, as if awaiting a courteous gesture or a warm smile to invite it across the threshold. It began with a silver breath on the windows each morning, a delicate frost that etched intricate, lacy patterns on the glass, like nature's own calligraphy. Then it started to wrap its tendrils around the corners of the shop, much like a tentative visitor uncertain of its welcome. It slipped between the pages of forgotten books, nestling in the quiet spaces, making them its own. And yet, rather than feeling like a loss or an ending, it felt like a beginning. A gentle transition, a subtle shift in life's rhythm.

It was a slowing down, reminiscent of the way the last few drops of honey take their time leaving the jar, savoring their own sweetness. It was also a deepening, similar to the rich hues of a sunset that linger on the horizon, painting the sky with colors that seem to hold secrets of the night to come. So, I made space for it, accepting the change, embracing the new pace. I allowed winter to settle in, to become a part of my daily rhythm, my breaths visible in the chilly air as I opened the shop each morning.

The room above the shop had long been half-used—part storage, part memory, part "I'll sort it eventually." It was a place where time seemed to stand still, where dust gathered undisturbed and memories lingered in every corner, like ghosts whispering stories from the past. But something within me stirred, a soft voice whispering that it was time to tend to this space. Not out of necessity or obligation, but out of hope, out of a desire to create something new and meaningful.

I cleared the space one afternoon while Aurelian was away, lending his skills to the grove-tenders who were enchanting the frostlines beyond the village. Whisker, my ever-present feline companion, supervised from a stack of dusty boxes, his tail flicking lazily as he watched me sort through forgotten tea jars filled with remnants of summers past. I found brittle spell scrolls, their magic still lingering like a faint perfume, whispering secrets of spells long cast. There was a coat I hadn't worn since before I understood what it meant to stay, to commit, to call a place home. It was like sifting through layers of my own life, each object a memory waiting to be rediscovered.

By the time dusk rolled in, the room had transformed. It wasn't perfect, with its rough edges and visible flaws, but it was lovingly crafted. A small bed now sat beneath the round window, inviting the soft glow of the setting sun to warm its coverlets. A writing desk was tucked into the corner, accompanied by a vase of dried winterbloom, their subtle scent filling the air like a promise of peace. A stack of extra quilts waited patiently, promising warmth and comfort on cold nights. A tiny enchanted lantern flickered like candlelight, casting dancing shadows even when unlit, as if magic itself was eager to inhabit the space, to breathe life into the quiet corners.

And on the nightstand, I placed the newest page from our shared book. Just one sentence, a testament to our journey, our growth, our love:

"We built this together—out of breath, and tea, and silence that listened back."

Aurelian returned as the day was fading, his hair windblown and cheeks pink from the cold. I met him at the door, kissed him once without a word, and led him upstairs. He took in the room slowly, his eyes lingering on each detail as if he didn't want to blink and miss a single moment of this revelation. His gaze traced the contours of the bed, the desk, the vase of winterbloom, as if each object was a word in a story he was reading for the first time.

Then he turned to me, his gaze soft and filled with wonder. "You made this?" he asked, his voice barely above a whisper, as if he was afraid to break the spell that had been cast over the room.

"We made this," I said, my voice steady with conviction. "Even if you didn't know you were helping, every moment we shared, every word we spoke, every silence we held—it all contributed to this."

He stepped into the room, his movements deliberate, almost reverent. He ran his fingers across the quilt, the lantern, the books tucked neatly along the shelf, as if each touch was a silent conversation, a thank you to the space that held our dreams. Each gesture was a acknowledgment of the love and care that had gone into creating this sanctuary.

"It feels like something new," he said, his voice filled with awe, as if he was standing on the precipice of a great discovery.

167

"It is," I whispered, stepping closer to him. "It's a room for winter. For staying. For us."

His eyes softened, and he reached out, tucking a strand of hair behind my ear, a tender gesture that spoke volumes. "For us," he echoed, a smile playing at the corners of his mouth, a promise of shared dreams and quiet moments.

He kissed me again—slow, grounding, warm enough to melt the frost around every worry I hadn't spoken aloud. It was a kiss that promised safety, that whispered of home and belonging. When we curled up under the blanket, Whisker hopping up to claim the end of the bed like a crown, I whispered into the quiet, "Let's not rush this."

"We never have," he murmured back, his arms tightening around me, a promise of shared tomorrows. "And we won't start now."

Downstairs, the shop hummed—content, unhurried, as if it too was settling into the rhythm of winter. The snow began to fall, each flake a gentle touch against the window, a soft whisper in the night. And for the first time in a long while, I didn't feel like something was ending. I felt like something was becoming. A new chapter was unfolding, a new season was beginning, and I was ready to embrace it all, to step into the dance of winter with an open heart and a willing spirit.

Chapter 25: A Room with Her Name On It

I didn't know she was making space for me. Not until the moment I stepped into the upstairs room and felt everything still—not because it was empty, but because it was ready. It was a stillness that seemed to whisper, inviting me to stay without demanding anything in return. The kind of stillness that asks nothing of you but to simply be present, to inhabit the space as if it were already yours.

Not until I stepped into the upstairs room did I truly understand. The window was open just enough to let the light filter in, casting a warm glow across the quilt she'd folded neatly at the edge of the bed. The sunlight softened the faded threads, giving them an almost ethereal quality. A lantern sat on the windowsill, unlit but humming faintly, as if it had already memorized the shape of her voice, waiting patiently to be ignited by her gentle touch.

The room was filled with books—of course there were books. But not in tidy, uniform stacks like those found in a shop display. These books were hers, each one carrying a piece of her story. Some were worn from frequent reading, their spines creased and pages dog-eared. Others were weathered, bearing the marks of time and adventure. Some were bookmarked with petals or curled parchment, reminders of moments captured in time. Among them, I recognized a few from days we'd shared downstairs, and others I hadn't seen since our time in the grove.

And there, on the desk, sat a mug. Not just any mug, but one of mine. The one she always let me use, a small but significant token of our shared moments. She hadn't built a shrine to our past; she had built a room, a sanctuary filled with warmth and windows that let in the soft, natural light. On the shelf, I noticed my favorite tea, a subtle but thoughtful touch that made the space feel even more welcoming.

Whisker had already claimed the chair, his presence adding a sense of familiarity and comfort to the room. The bed wasn't made to impress; it was made to hold us, to be a place of rest and refuge. That's when I knew. I hadn't just stayed in Faerrow; I'd been kept, embraced, and welcomed into a world that felt like home.

When she led me up the stairs, I tried to play it steady, to maintain a calm exterior despite the emotions welling up inside me. I tried not to show how my chest ached the way roots do when they find soil that says yes, when they find a place to grow and thrive. She didn't say much either, her words few but powerful.

Just: "We made this."

And somehow, that was everything. Those three words encapsulated the effort, the love, and the intent behind the room she had created for us. I kissed her slowly, the kind of kiss that says thank you. The kind that says I see this—not just the bed and the books and the light—but the courage it took to let me into her world without asking for a single thing in return.

Later, when she fell asleep with her head tucked beneath my chin, Whisker curled at our feet, I lay there thinking. She didn't ask me to belong; she let me choose to. She gave me the space to decide, to find my place in her world, and in doing so, she made it feel like home.

Chapter 26: The Spell Behind the Fire

Midwinter always carried a scent like no other, a blend of cinnamon and old paper that permeated the air, subtle yet unmistakable. It didn't arrive in dramatic storms or sudden changes, but rather in gentle, incremental shifts that slowly transformed the world. Frost began to cling to the ground, no longer melting away by noon, and the trees, once whispering with the wind, fell silent as if listening to the hush that descended upon the land. The breeze carried a new crispness, and the sun cast long shadows, painting the landscape in muted hues of blue and gray. Even the tea blends seemed to steep slower, as if the magic itself wanted to take a moment to rest and rejuvenate, infusing the air with comforting aromas that promised warmth and respite.

In Faerrow, Midwinter wasn't merely a holiday marked on the calendar. It was a pause, a moment of respite from the relentless march of time. A chance for the world and its inhabitants to take a breath, to reflect, and to find solace in the quietude. It was a season of introspection, a time when the lines between the magical and the mundane blurred, and the world sighed in anticipation of renewal. This year, I wanted the shop to embody that spirit—a sanctuary where one could find peace amidst the subtle magic of the season, a haven that offered comfort and warmth against the encroaching chill.

Aurelian and I spent the morning meticulously stringing garlands of dried orange slices and silverberry sprigs across the rafters. The shop was filled with the sweet, tangy scent of citrus and the earthy aroma of the berries, creating a warm and inviting atmosphere that seemed to wrap around us like a familiar embrace. Whisker, our feline companion, chased the ribbons with an air of dignified chaos, his tail flicking with excitement as he darted between our feet. He pounced on stray leaves and batted at the orange slices, his antics adding a lightheartedness to our work. I charmed the lanterns to flicker a bit brighter, casting a soft glow that bathed the shop in hues of soft white and honey-gold, the colors of hearthlight and closeness, chasing away the shadows that lingered in the corners.

As we moved the hearth rug to sweep away the dust and debris, Aurelian paused, his attention caught by something unusual. I turned to see what had captured his interest, my hands still clutching the worn fabric of the rug. He was kneeling at the fireplace, his fingers tracing the grooves of a stone I'd walked past countless times without ever really noticing. The stone bore a faint knotwork pattern carved into its surface, a design I'd never given much thought to before. It was just another part of the shop's old architecture, or so I thought.

"What's this?" Aurelian asked, his voice filled with curiosity, his eyes reflecting the dim light of the nearby lantern.

"It's just part of the foundation," I replied, brushing flour dust from my sleeve, my mind still half-focused on the task at hand. "Nothing special, as far as I know. Just another stone in an old building."

"No," he murmured, his brow furrowed in concentration, his fingers lingering on the intricate carvings. "It's a sigil."

He pressed his palm firmly against the stone, and the air in the room seemed to shift subtly, as if responding to his touch. It was a barely perceptible change, like the first breath of wind before a storm, a gentle stirring that whispered of hidden magic.

The stone began to glow, only faintly at first, like a spark remembering it had once been a flame. Then, with a quiet click, a hidden compartment within the hearth opened, revealing a single sheet of parchment. The parchment was old but remarkably well-preserved,

175

its edges slightly yellowed with age. The ink scrawled across it was in a hand that stopped my breath—my father's. The sight of his familiar script sent a jolt through me, a mix of nostalgia and longing that I hadn't felt in years.

I unfolded the parchment slowly, my heart pounding in my chest, my fingers trembling slightly. The page held a spell, but not one of power or protection. It was a spell for dwelling, a spell to root the soul where the body lives, to invite belonging, and to let the quiet become home. The instructions were clear and concise, written in my father's steady hand: Use sparingly. Only where love intends to stay.

I stared at the spell for a long time, my mind racing with thoughts and memories. Aurelian didn't speak; he simply moved to stand beside me, his hands gentle and comforting on my back, his presence a silent support that grounded me in the moment. The shop around us seemed to hold its breath, waiting for the magic to unfold.

"He built this into the foundation," I whispered, my voice filled with a mix of awe and sadness, the realization settling over me like a warm cloak. My father had left a piece of himself here, a gift hidden in the heart of the shop, waiting for me to find it.

"You were never meant to be untethered," Aurelian said softly, his voice a gentle reassurance in the quiet of the room. "Even when he couldn't stay, he wanted you to have a place to belong."

I nodded, tears pricking at the corners of my eyes but not falling, a lump forming in my throat. Then, with a deep breath, I stood and read the spell aloud, my voice steady and clear, the words resonating through the shop like a melody long forgotten.

The shop didn't flash or flicker. There was no dramatic swirl of wind, no glowing symbols or thundering roots. Instead, there was just… a warmth. A settling. It was as if every brick, every beam, every book in the shop breathed deeper, as if the very essence of the place recognized me as something permanent, a part of its soul. The air seemed to hum with a gentle energy, a soft vibration that whispered of belonging and home.

And in that moment, I recognized myself too. I felt a connection to the shop, to Faerrow, that ran deeper than I had ever imagined. It was a sense of belonging, of being rooted in a place that was truly home, a place where my heart could rest and my soul could flourish. The realization filled me with a profound sense of peace, a quiet joy that settled over me like the first snowfall of winter.

177

That night, Aurelian and I sat in front of the fire—a real fire now, steady and slow, its flames dancing and flickering, casting a warm glow over the room. The fire crackled softly, a comforting sound that filled the silence between us. Aurelian placed his hand over mine, his touch firm and reassuring, a promise of steadfastness and love.

"I'm not going anywhere," he said, his voice filled with conviction, his eyes reflecting the warmth of the fire.

"I know," I whispered, my heart full of everything soft and certain, a sense of security and contentment that I hadn't known before. "Neither am I."

He reached into his coat and pulled out our book, a worn volume filled with memories and dreams, its pages yellowed with age and use. He opened it to the last page and, with careful strokes, wrote a single line: Not a vow. Not a spell. Just a truth we're still writing.

I leaned into him, feeling the warmth of his body against mine, and as snow brushed gently against the windows, painting the world outside in a blanket of white, I finally believed it: I wasn't just part of Faerrow anymore. It was part of me, a piece of my heart and soul, a place where I belonged, where I was rooted, where I was home.

Chapter 27: A Quiet Yes

The snow had fallen overnight in a heavy, unceasing cascade, as if the sky itself were weary with the burden of winter. Each flake was thick and lazy, meandering its way to the ground, painting the world in a pristine white that seemed to slow time to a crawl. Faerrow, ordinarily a bustling town filled with the cacophony of daily life, now lay hushed and still, blanketed beneath winter's gentle touch. Every rooftop and cobblestone was rounded and softened, their edges blunted by the snow's embrace. Trees stood sentinel, their branches laden with white, holding their breath beneath the hush of winter's gentle hand. The silence was profound, almost reverent, turning even the slightest sound into an intrusion on the peaceful scene.

I stood at the window, a cup of warm tea cradled in my hands, the steam rising lazily in the chill air. The shop around me was still asleep, the usual hum of activity replaced by a tranquil stillness that felt almost magical. This was not a morning to be rushed through, but one to be savored, a morning that asked for quiet introspection rather than hurried action. It was a morning that seemed to beckon for an answer to questions left unspoken, a gentle nudge toward reflection and contemplation.

There, tucked beneath my teacup, was a small, unassuming note folded neatly in half. There was no wax seal, no intricate spellwork to guard its contents—just Aurelian's handwriting, small and steady, as if each letter had been written with a deliberate calm. The words were simple, yet they held a weight that was impossible to ignore, a gravity that seemed to pull at the very core of me.

If you still want slowness, meet me in the grove. Bring only what you'd miss. And say nothing unless it's true.

It wasn't a grand proposal, not the kind that people made with rings or grand declarations. It was something far gentler, far more intimate. A request for presence, a question written in the quiet spaces between words. It was an invitation to share a moment, to be present in a way that went beyond mere physical proximity. An invitation to let go of the noise and the hurry, and to simply be.

I didn't overthink it. Instead, I moved with a kind of certainty that felt both new and familiar, a sense of purpose that seemed to guide my every action. I packed only what mattered: our book, its pages filled with shared memories and dreams, the corners worn with time and love; my favorite cardigan, soft and comfortable, a testament to the years it had spent wrapped around me; Whisker, who insisted on coming by hopping into my satchel and refusing to leave, his tiny body warm against my side; and a single slip of parchment, blank and waiting, because not all beginnings needed words to define them.

The path to the grove was quieter than ever, the usual sounds of the forest muffled by the thick blanket of snow. The crunch of my boots on the fresh powder was the only sound that accompanied me, a steady rhythm that seemed to echo the beat of my heart. Even the trees seemed to be waiting, their branches bowed under the weight of the snow and something that felt eerily like hope. I walked slowly, allowing the cold to kiss my cheeks and the silence to press into me like a comforting embrace. Each step was deliberate, each breath measured, as if the very air around me was charged with anticipation.

When I reached the clearing, he was already there. No cloak to shield him from the cold, no fire to warm his hands—just Aurelian, standing in the center of the grove. Behind him, the heart-tree glowed faintly beneath a layer of frost, its branches reaching out like welcoming arms. He didn't move as I approached, didn't speak. He simply held out his hand, an invitation that felt as natural as breathing.

181

I took it, and in that moment, I knew this was the life I'd been writing toward all along. Not in sudden, dramatic turns, not in sweeping, grandiose changes. But in the soft, persistent choice to say yes to the quiet things, to the moments that whispered rather than shouted, to the love that grew slowly and steadily, like the roots of the heart-tree. It was a love that didn't need grand gestures or loud proclamations, but one that thrived in the silent spaces, in the small, everyday moments that made up a life.

We sat beneath the heart-tree together, shoulder to shoulder, our hands entwined. The world around us seemed to hold its breath, the silence broken only by the soft rustling of the trees and the distant whisper of the wind. Without ceremony, without fanfare, I reached for our book, turning to a fresh page. The parchment was smooth beneath my fingertips, the ink flowing easily as I wrote a single word:

Yes.

He didn't ask what it meant. He didn't need to. He pressed a kiss to my temple, slow and warm, a gesture that held a thousand unspoken words. And whispered, "Then I will stay as long as you let me."

The snow continued to fall, each flake a silent promise of the future. The grove held us gently, its embrace protective and nurturing. And the future we hadn't yet written curled quietly between us, waiting—like everything else in Faerrow—for the right moment to bloom. The world around us was still, but within that stillness, there was a sense of anticipation, a quiet excitement for the chapters yet to be written, for the love that would grow and flourish beneath the watchful eyes of the heart-tree. It was a love that promised to be as enduring and as steady as the ancient tree that stood guard over us, a love that would weather the storms and the silences, the seasons and the years. A love that was, in every way, a quiet, profound yes.

Epilogue

What We Built in the Quiet

Four Months Later, Early Spring - Elowen

It's always the sound of the kettle that gets me. Not the chirping of the birds as they welcome the dawn, not the steady hum of the river as it carves its way through the landscape once more, not even the first determined bud pushing its way through the softened earth, defying the remnants of winter. No, it's the gentle, soothing whistle of water heating on the hearth that truly signals the start of the day.

That sound means someone is home. It means that someone is attending to the small, everyday tasks that make up a life. It means that the world has not crumbled away in the night, that it is still turning, still breathing, still alive. Most importantly, it means that I am still here, still a part of this world, still living and breathing alongside it.

Faerrow blooms slowly, almost languidly, and this year, it's blooming with us in it, like we're a part of its very heart. The snow that had blanketed the village melted away last week, leaving the ground damp and the air crisp. The lanterns that had been frozen in the trees, their glass panes coated with ice, now hang freely once more. They sway gently in the breeze, casting soft, dancing shadows on the ground below. The bakery down the street reopened its back patio, filling the air with the scent of fresh bread and sweet pastries. Children laugh and play, chalking runes onto the cobblestones—runes that mean nothing and yet, somehow, everything.

Aurelian has taken to waking earlier than I do now. He starts the tea, the scent of it filling the room, and stokes the fire, the crackle of the flames a comforting soundtrack to the morning. Sometimes, I wake to the smell of thyme or the lingering scent of smoke from the fire. Other times, it's the fresh, green scent of pressed clover from his latest foraging trip. And sometimes, just sometimes, I wake to him pressing a soft kiss to my shoulder, whispering something that never quite makes it into the air, like a secret meant only for the two of us.

We keep a jar by the door now. It's not for memory slips, not for the things we want to forget. No, this jar is for beginnings.

185

Whenever something starts—a new blend of tea, a new idea, a new dream—we write it down on a slip of paper. We fold it once, carefully, deliberately, and drop it into the jar. We'll read them all at the year's turn, a celebration of the things that have begun, the things that have grown. But I think we already know what most of them say. I think we already know the dreams we're chasing, the lives we're building.

The shop is thriving, but not in a loud, boisterous way. No, it's thriving in that quiet, secret sort of way that feels almost magical. People come not just for the books, but for what happens around them. For the slowness of a lazy afternoon, for the warmth of a steaming cup of tea on a cold day. For the conversations that spring up between strangers, for the connections that are forged over shared stories.

I never thought I'd love being seen. I never thought I'd crave the feeling of eyes on me, of being truly, wholly noticed. But Aurelian never stares. He simply notices. He notices when my shoulders are tight with tension, when my voice softens with joy or wonder. He notices when I reach for certain mugs on certain days, when I seek comfort or familiarity. He sees me as I am—always in motion, always becoming, always growing and changing. And he never asks me to be

186

anything else. He never asks me to be still, to be quiet, to be small. He simply lets me be, and in that, I find a freedom I never knew I needed.

Today, I found a sprout curling up between the floorboards behind the counter. A real one, not just a metaphor or a dream. It was tiny, with green leaves no bigger than a fingertip, but it was there. It was real. I knelt down, whispered a blessing over it, and left it be. Some things root themselves, whether we invite them or not. They find their place in the world and they grow, despite the odds, despite the challenges.

But some things—we choose. We choose them every day, with every breath, with every heartbeat. Like Aurelian. Like this shop. Like love, slow and certain, steady and sure. We choose them, and in doing so, we build a life. We build a story.

I poured two cups of tea, the liquid hot and fragrant, and stood at the window while the morning opened around us. The village woke up, the grove came to life, the shop breathed in the new day. All of it breathing. All of it ours. And I thought, not for the first time, that I didn't find a story to live in. I built one. I built it with my own two hands, with my own heart, with my own soul. And it was beautiful. It was mine. It was home.

* * *

The Rooted Kind of Love

Early Spring, Faerrow - Aurelian

I used to think love was movement, a restless energy that lived in the chase. That it thrived on the thrill of pursuit, knowing precisely what to strive for, how far to reach, and what to release in order to follow someone into the untamed wilderness. It was an endless dance, a breathless journey that never seemed to find its destination.

But that was before her.

Before the quaint bookshop called Thistle & Thread beckoned me with a whisper more powerful than any enchantment. Before a girl with fingers stained by ink and stories pressed a warm cup of tea into my hands, offering a silence so profound it left me unsure of how to reciprocate.

Elowen never asked me to stay. She didn't bind me with promises or pleas. Instead, she created a space beside her, an invitation subtle and silent, waiting to see if I would choose to fill it. And I did. Not because the roads had worn me out, not because my spirit was

188

weary of wandering. But because, for the first time in my life, I yearned to be remembered in the place where I stood.

The grove still calls me, its rustling leaves and ancient secrets tugging at my heart. So does the earth, the rich soil that cradles life, the tea leaves that hold stories in their fragrant steam, and the work that grounds me. But now, every seed I plant carries her voice within it. Every blend I mix holds a warmth I only learned because she handed it to me in a chipped moon-cup, her eyes knowing and kind, telling me it was just what I needed.

She was right, as she so often is.

I watch her sometimes when she doesn't know I'm looking. She hums softly to the books as she shelves them, her voice a gentle lullaby for the stories they hold. She murmurs to Whisker, our feline companion, treating him as part oracle, part co-owner of our little sanctuary. She writes tiny spells into the corners of recipe cards, her magic quiet and unassuming, never seeking attention or recognition.

She thinks her magic is subtle, a soft whisper in the wind. But it has remade my life, reshaped the very foundations of who I am. We keep a jar by the window now—our jar for beginnings. She writes on parchment, her words flowing like a river across the page. I etch things onto bark, my markings rough and earthy, a testament to the roots that have grown deep within me. Neither of us shares what we've added until the thaw, when the world awakens from its slumber.

But I already know what mine will say.

"Love isn't what follows you, chasing after your heels. It's what roots beside you, standing firm and steady, and stays until spring."

And me? I'm still here. Still waking to the sound of her breath beside me, a rhythm as steady and comforting as the heartbeat of the earth itself. Still home, in the room we built together, in the life she allowed me to grow into. In the kind of love that doesn't shout its presence from the rooftops, but still echoes through every fiber of my being, resonating with a quiet, steady strength that will endure through all seasons.

Acknowledgments

Stories may begin in quiet corners, but they never grow alone.

To my daughters, Grace and Ashlyn—your magic lives in every line. Thank you for being my joy, my muses, my wild-hearted wonders.

To the early readers and kindred spirits who believed in this story before it had a spine—your encouragement lit lanterns when I needed them most.

To the writers, readers, and dreamers who create soft places for others to land—you inspire me daily.

And to the quiet: the pages we reread, the tea left steeping, the friends who linger after the last word—thank you. This book is for you.

With   all   my   heart,

Katherine Kuehnel

Author's Note

When I began *Thistle & Thread*, I didn't set out to write a grand adventure or a sweeping epic. I wanted to write a love story that didn't rush. One where the heart didn't demand or prove—but softened, deepened, and stayed.

This story is for anyone who's ever made themselves small to protect something quiet. For those who carry tenderness like armor. For the ones who find peace in slowness, in rituals, in quiet places made sacred simply by care.

It's also for my daughters, Grace and Ashlyn—who remind me that magic isn't always fire and flight. Sometimes it's a steady hand. A kind word. A room made ready before the guest arrives. Sometimes, magic is simply being seen and loved without being asked to change.

Thank you for stepping into Faerrow, into Elowen's world. I hope you find something here that lingers gently with you—like a whisper, or a warm light left on.

With love,
Katherine Kuehnel

About the Author

Katherine Kuehnel writes cozy fantasy stories where love lingers gently, magic is brewed alongside tea, and quiet hearts find a place to belong.

A mother to two bright and magical daughters, Grace and Ashlyn, Katherine lives in a world of bedtime stories, spontaneous dance parties, and book piles that keep growing. She's fueled by good coffee, long walks under changing leaves, and the belief that softness is a strength.

When not writing, you can find her curled up with a romantasy or cozy romance novel, browsing bookstores with no intention of leaving empty-handed, or snuggling her black cat, Salem—who insists on supervising every page.

Thistle & Thread is her debut novel—and a quiet celebration of tenderness, rooted hearts, and the slow, sacred magic of being known.

Follow her journey at @cozywithkatherine on Instagram.

✦ Coming Soon from Katherine Kuehnel

The Honeybrew Café

In Faerrow, the seasons turn like pages, and the village wakes to the scent of cinnamon, honey, and something new.

Hazel Thorne has always dreamed of running a place where warmth lingers in every cup. The Honeybrew Café is her heart stitched into brick and wood—cozy tables, jars of wildflower honey, and the calico cat who believes she owns the place.

She isn't expecting Elias—the wanderer with dark curls, a knack for jam-making, and eyes that feel like home. But when the rhythm of Hazel's café life begins to entwine with his, the two must decide if they are brave enough to stay—not just in Faerrow, but with each other.

🍯 A story of cinnamon mornings, honey-sweet promises, and love that grows where you least expect it.

Coming soon...

Made in United States
North Haven, CT
05 October 2025

80450663R00118